# Mayor Mayhem:
## She ran for office and took out corruption with a safe word.

**Written by: by Jordan Wright, M.Ed. & Ibrahim Roble**

# Copyright Page

Mayor Mayhem: She Ran for Office and Took Out Corruption with a Safe Word

For permissions or bulk orders, contact:
Jordan.Wright@humbolton.com or
Ibrahim.Roble@Humbolton.com

First Edition: July 2025

Cover design by Jordan Wright, M.Ed.

ISBN: 978-1-966703-08-2

Printed in the United States of America

# Table of Contents

# Chapter 1: The Clap Heard 'Round the Hood

### BBQ Breakdown – Tyrone's "Speech"

Dusty Springs, Georgia, was not the kind of place where enlightenment happened by accident. It was the kind of place where car rims cost more than college, gossip traveled faster than Amazon Prime, and every backyard baby shower ended in at least one fistfight or paternity question. Today was no different.

The grill was smoking, the bounce house was sagging like a pastor's promise, and Tyrone Jenkins was standing on a wobbly white folding chair, shirtless, sauced, and clutching a rib like it was a microphone sent by God Himself.

"Listen up, y'all!" he shouted, greasy fingers waving over a crowd of folding chairs, paper plates, and disinterested cousins. "I got somethin' to say. Real talk. From the heart."

Several people looked up, mostly because the music had dipped and someone had unplugged the Bluetooth speaker to charge their vape. A few phones rose into the air. Dusty Springs didn't get many TED Talks, and even fewer that started with the speaker holding a Corona beer and a baby bottle simultaneously.

"We out here celebratin' life, right? But lemme tell you somethin'… COVID? That sh*t fake. Made up. Manufactured by the government to control y'all minds and put microchips in your bloodstream."

"Here we go," muttered Cousin DeRay, adjusting his do-rag and reaching for another chicken wing.

"See, y'all out here wearin' masks like fools, lettin' these nurses inject you with who-knows-what. Not me. I got protection." Tyrone patted the drawstring of his gym shorts proudly. "I got crystals. Chakra-charged from my girl Cinnamon. That's why I ain't never been sick."

There was a pause. Somewhere, a baby started crying. Probably from embarrassment.

"I got tiger's eye by my nuts, rose quartz under my mattress, and I sleep with amethyst in my durag. Ain't no virus touchin' me. I'm spiritually boosted, baby!"

"Spiritually boosted?" someone echoed, followed by the kind of laugh you try to stifle and absolutely fail.

That's when the crowd parted like gossip at a family funeral, and in walked **Tierra Jenkins**, carrying a clipboard, a zip-lock bag of antibiotics, and the exhausted look of a woman who had been cleaning up after this fool since Obama's first term.

She wore her scrubs like armor, her Nikes like weapons, and her expression like she was already regretting not filing taxes as single.

"Sit your dumb ass down, Tyrone."

Tyrone blinked, the bravado slipping a bit. "Baby, wait, I was just tryna drop knowledge—"

"You dropped something, alright. And it wasn't knowledge. It was gonorrhea. Again."

The crowd exploded. Someone choked on potato salad. A phone dropped. An auntie made the sign of the cross.

Tyrone gripped the back of his neck like he could massage the shame away. "Why you gotta air me out like that?"

"Because I told you to get tested. You said crystals would 'vibe out the bacteria.' Crystals, Tyrone? Really?"

"It's all energy, baby—"

"Energy don't burn when you pee."

She held up the test results like it was the Ten Commandments. "You've got an STI, and I'm ninety percent sure you also have delusions of grandeur and a mild-to-severe TikTok addiction. And don't try to blame Cinnamon. She had a yeast infection, not an STD—*you* were the common denominator."

"I thought that was a symptom of ascension!"

"Your penis is not on a spiritual journey. It's infected."

A heavy silence fell across the yard, except for someone whispering, "Daaaaaamn," like it was a BET Awards roast.

Tyrone slid off the chair slowly, like a decommissioned statue of a fallen general. His pride hit the grass before his feet did.

Tierra shook her head, turned to the audience, and raised a hand like she was running a seminar.

"For everyone who heard this man say COVID is fake, please note: He also believes you can cure rashes with peppermint tea and foot rubs. This is not a reliable source."

Aunt Charlene fanned herself with a church bulletin. "Is this still the baby shower?"

"Yes," Tierra said flatly. "And if y'all keep sharing forks and denying science, the next one will be a funeral."

Then, as if summoned by sheer absurdity, **Cinnamon** stepped out from the shadows of the garage wearing a matching sage-green headwrap and kimono set, clutching a velvet pouch full of what she called "chakra stabilizers." She had glitter on her

7

cheeks and a ring light in her purse, just in case enlightenment demanded a livestream.

She didn't say a word. She just lit an incense stick, waved it in Tyrone's direction, and whispered, "Cleanse him, ancestors. He knoweth not what toxins he carry."

Tierra blinked once, long and slow. "Girl, unless those ancestors come with a prescription pad, get your patchouli ass off this lawn."

The crowd erupted again. Someone shouted, "Worldstar!" and Cinnamon calmly pulled out her phone and began recording her own rebuttal TikTok. Tyrone, hunched now like a child who just realized detention was real, tried to slink toward the cooler without making eye contact.

Tierra watched him go, hands on her hips.

"And somebody better Clorox that chair."

Fade out on the baby crying again.

### Medical Dragging

### POV: Tierra Jenkins

Tierra didn't walk into the party—she **stormed** in like she'd just clocked out of hell, which was to say, **the ER.**

She hadn't planned to come. She'd spent her whole morning stitching up a man who got bit by his girlfriend's emotional support iguana. She still had a line of patients waiting back at County Hospital who thought turmeric could cure sepsis. But then her phone lit up like a Christmas tree and started pinging:

8

"Girl, your man on Live again."
"Tyrone talkin' about chakra nuts."
"Ain't this yo baby daddy?"

She paused her lunch—a slightly squished sandwich and an unlabeled bottle of orange stuff she suspected was energy drink and regret—and headed over with the clipboard, the antibiotics, and the kind of patience that only someone trained in trauma triage could possess.

Now she stood in front of Tyrone, crowd watching, ribs half-eaten, gossip hanging heavier than the humidity.

She didn't flinch. Didn't blink. Just took a deep, nurse-initiated breath and went in for the kill.

"You stood up on that chair," she said, coolly, "shirtless, smelling like smoked lies and bad decisions, to tell our friends and family that COVID is fake... *again*."

Tyrone opened his mouth to explain. She shut it for him with a single raised finger.

"Let me walk the room through some facts. Since apparently, we're all in science class now."

She paced a slow circle, holding the clipboard like it was a sacred tablet of shame.

"Fact one. Tyrone has, at this very moment, an active case of gonorrhea, confirmed by urine culture, discharge analysis, and his complete inability to say the word 'burning' without clenching."

The crowd gasped. Someone dropped a Dixie cup of peach punch. A toddler screamed just because.

"Fact two," she continued, with the rhythm of a TED Talk and the ferocity of Judge Judy off her meds, "this is the third time in

9

six months that he's come into my clinic claiming a rash was due to a 'chakra detox.' You cannot detox your dick with eucalyptus."

"Third?" Tyrone croaked, confused.

"Third that *you* know about. I count the urgent care visit you tried to make under the name 'Tyquavious J.' at that clinic in Decatur."

More gasps. A snort. Maybe an Amen.

"Fact three. He told the nurse practitioner that he was abstinent. While she was swabbing him. And humming 'WAP.'"

Tyrone looked like he was trying to shrink into his own shadow. But Tierra wasn't done. Not by half.

She pulled out a little plastic bottle and shook it like a maraca of accountability.

"This here? This is azithromycin. That's an antibiotic, for those of you who skipped high school or think essential oils can treat infections. Tyrone was supposed to take it yesterday. Instead, he said—direct quote—'I was gonna wait until Mercury stopped retrograding.'"

Someone wheezed. Someone else whispered, "She a whole menace."

"And that, ladies and gentlemen, is why you're all sitting near an infected man who still believes burning sage will clean his urinary tract."

The silence was exquisite. A sauce-drenched hush of barbecue-stained guilt.

"And Cinnamon..." she turned, slowly, until her eyes found the side chick, who had just lit another stick of incense and was whispering into her iPhone like a third-tier medium on a discounted spirit plan, "...your spiritual cleansing ain't cleansing sh*t."

Cinnamon's mouth opened, indignant.

Tierra held up a test strip. "Yeast infection. Not spiritual trauma. No amount of praying over yogurt is going to cure what monistat can."

Cinnamon recoiled like someone had just smacked her with a sacred scroll.

"You got your followers thinking lemon water and positive affirmations will protect them from disease," Tierra snapped. "Meanwhile, your pH is staging a rebellion."

A cheer rose from the crowd. A slow, steady clap started from the elderly cousin with a portable oxygen tank and a sequined visor. Even the bounce house stopped wheezing for a second, like it needed to process what it just heard.

Tyrone, for his part, looked like he wanted the earth to swallow him. Not from embarrassment—he was used to being loud and wrong—but because **this time, he couldn't talk his way out of it**. Tierra had facts, printouts, and the righteous wrath of every exhausted woman who'd ever dated potential instead of people.

She turned to the crowd.

"If any of y'all believe him over a licensed medical professional, please leave now and go gargle hand sanitizer before you reproduce."

A few people shuffled nervously. No one left.

She snapped her gloves off. "And somebody clean that chair. It's contaminated."

She didn't wait for applause. She walked straight to the cooler, cracked open a ginger ale, and took a sip like she'd just exorcised a demon.

Behind her, the baby started crying again.

## Cinnamon's TikTok Madness

### POV: Cinnamon Laveau

Cinnamon adjusted the ring light so it caught the glitter just right on her cheekbones. Lighting was sacred. Angle was divine. A shadow in the wrong place and the whole reading would lose its spiritual resonance—or worse, its engagement rate.

She took a breath, centered her energy, and hit record.

"Grand rising, my babies," she whispered, pressing her hands together like prayer met performance. "Welcome back to *Vibrations & Validation with Cinnamon*—the only place where healing meets hot girl vibes."

Soft flute music played from her iPad, looping behind her voice like the soundtrack of an overpriced yoga retreat. Behind her, her spiritual altar sat in all its dollar-store glory: a crooked candle labeled *Wealth Manifestation*, a dried bundle of sage tied with a shoelace, and a statue of Oshun holding a plastic wine glass filled with pineapple soda.

"I know y'all saw what happened at the barbecue," she said solemnly, like she was addressing a nation in mourning. "Tyrone's auric field was fully compromised. The masculine divine is *under attack*, and we, as feminine vessels of healing, must respond. With grace. With love. And with this sponsored yoni detox kit, link in bio."

She leaned closer to the camera, giving her best concerned high priestess face.

"He didn't infect me, y'all. He was *already infected*. Spiritually. By jealousy. By fear. By that nurse girlfriend of his, Tierra, who refuses to let her third eye open. Baby, you got a stethoscope, not a soul."

She laughed, gently, as if she were teaching a toddler that gravity exists.

"I ain't mad at her, though. I'm just ahead on my journey. She'll get there. Once she cleanses her womb of all that masculine ego energy. I can help with that too—DM me."

She paused to strike a pose while pretending to write in her manifestation journal. Really, it was a grocery list, but on camera, anything with cursive and crystals looked divine.

"As for Tyrone," she continued, "yes, I did lay with him—because Spirit told me to. Sometimes, we gotta enter the lion's den to rebalance the pride. But that's also why I'm launching my new course: *Sexual Alchemy for Hood Healers.*"

She held up a laminated flyer.

**TOPICS INCLUDE:**

- Energy Cleansing After Community D***
- Chakra Checkups: How to Tell if His Root Is Rotten
- Manifesting Loyalty with Moonwater and Boundaries (and Block Buttons)
- Live Ceremony: Reclaiming Your Power from Toxic Dudes Named Tyrone

She winked. "Only $199. Payment plans accepted. EBT if it's the spiritual kind."

The comments rolled in on her screen like gospel:

*"YES QUEEN"*
*"She went there! Tierra who???"*
*"Where can I get the yoni detox crystal again?"*

Cinnamon flipped her waist-length faux locs over her shoulder and lit another stick of incense. The smoke curled dramatically, as if the ancestors were on cue.

She reached behind her and picked up a rose quartz egg from a satin-lined box and cradled it like a Fabergé truth bomb.

"This is what y'all need," she said, serious now. "When you get spiritually burned, you gotta fight back with love, herbs, and inner pH alignment."

She stood and backed up, revealing she was wearing a sheer pink robe, fuzzy slippers, and boy shorts that read **"WOKE AF"** in rhinestones.

Then, with one last piercing stare into the camera:

"To the man who gave me the clap... may your energy be reclaimed. May your crystals break in the dryer. And may every side chick you chase after send you right back to me, healed and humbled."

She blew a kiss.

"Catch me live tonight at 7. We're doing a collective card pull for the community—and exposing fake nurses with dusty chakras. Love and light, baby. Love. And. Light."

She ended the recording and exhaled.

Her roommate peeked in through the door. "You done?"

"Just finished," Cinnamon said, already uploading it with ten hashtags and a filter named "Celestial Glow." "Can you grab my gold cauldron? I'm about to go viral again."

The roommate raised an eyebrow. "Ain't that the popcorn bowl?"

"Not when I'm channeling, it's not."

She turned back to the screen and watched the view count climb.

## Mistress Maybelline Takes the Call

### POV: Nana May Jackson

The living room was quiet, save for the faint groan of rope tightening against regret.

Nana May Jackson—grandmother, former lunch lady, and reigning queen of Dusty Springs' underground discipline scene—sat serenely in her recliner. A floral housecoat covered her frame, her slippers puffed with lavender stuffing, and her perfectly pressed wig gleamed beneath the soft light of a dusty chandelier. She looked every inch the sweet old Southern woman. The lace doilies on the armrest even matched her pistol holster.

Across the room, kneeling on a crocheted mat, was a man in a city utility vest and a ball gag that read *"Ego in Time-Out."*

"You missed your payment," she said calmly, sipping her chamomile tea. "That wasn't very wise, was it, baby?"

The man whimpered something through the gag. She waved it off.

"No, don't speak. You had your chance when I warned you not to reroute the storm drain budget into your golf tournament. What did you think I'd do? Bake you a forgiveness pie?"

She stood, stretched, and walked behind him. The click of her orthopedic heels on tile echoed like a gavel in a courtroom no one dared contest. She wasn't angry. Nana May never got angry. She simply corrected the world with unwavering precision.

She pulled the red rope just enough to make the man squirm. Not from pain, but from the unbearable weight of his own conscience finally being held accountable.

That's when her phone rang.

She glanced at the screen: **Tyrone.**

Her sigh was a symphony of disappointment, arthritis, and blood pressure management.

"Pause," she told the kneeler. "You stay there and meditate on every tax dollar you misappropriated."

She picked up the phone and sank back into the recliner.

"What?" she asked, with no grandmotherly softness at all.

The voice on the other end came fast, panicked, and too loud. "Grandma—Nana—it's bad. It's real bad. Tierra said I got a... a thing. Like a real thing. Like an antibiotic thing. And she went all *Grey's Anatomy* in front of everybody. In front of *Auntie Dora*, Nana!"

"I know what that means," Nana said, calmly sipping her tea. "Tierra wouldn't make a scene unless you deserved it. What'd you do this time? And don't you lie—I still got that sixth sense."

"I didn't lie! I just… reinterpreted reality for my mental alignment."

"Boy, you better shut your metaphysical mouth."

"I think I'm dying."

"You thought COVID was a hologram projected by satellites. You'll live. You just got roasted with facts, and now your spirit's inflamed."

Tyrone whimpered. It was impressive—he sounded like the kneeling man across the room. Must've been hereditary.

"Grandma, can I come over?"

"No. I've got a client in spiritual time-out. Come by tomorrow. Bring wipes."

"But Tierra called me a vector. She said I'm a threat to the community!"

"Well. You are."

"Grandma!"

"I told you when you were eight not to stick your pecker where your purpose ain't welcome. You didn't listen then, and you sure as hell ain't evolved since."

He groaned. "You always gotta hit me with lessons when I'm vulnerable?"

"That's the only time you actually shut up long enough to learn."

There was a silence on the line. Then, softly, "I think I need help."

Nana stared out the window. The pecan tree was shedding like a drunk stripper on Arbor Day. The news was playing low in the background. A city official was giving a press conference, sweat glistening under cheap makeup, as reporters grilled him about misused COVID relief funds.

"Help is earned," she said finally. "And yours is comin'. But not the kind you want. I gotta go."

"Nana, wait—"

She ended the call and set the phone down on a crocheted coaster that read *Reclaiming My Time* in glitter thread.

Across the room, her client whimpered.

Nana turned to him, her voice warm and terrifying.

"Now where were we?"

He moaned behind the gag, softly. She untied the rope with one smooth pull, letting him collapse gently to the ground like a crumbling policy paper.

"Time's up," she said. "Your penance is done."

He nodded, sweaty and grateful, bowing like a man in church who had just been granted reprieve from the wrath of the Lord.

"Payment envelope's on the counter," she reminded him. "And if you ever reroute my water bill into another nonprofit brunch, I'll post the video of you crying in a leash on city council's Facebook page."

"Yes, Mistress," he said, barely audible.

"Good boy."

He let himself out. Nana moved to the window and watched the mayor's face on the TV screen morph from smug to stuttering. The news chyron rolled past.

**BREAKING: Dusty Springs Under Fire for Pandemic Mismanagement. Pothole Relief Fund Mysteriously Missing.**

Her hand reached for the tea, then stopped.

She picked up her tablet, blew the dust off, and opened the Notes app. A new line appeared at the top:

**Things That Need Whipping:**

- Tyrone's judgment
- Cinnamon's spiritual hustle
- Tierra's patience (rewarded with wine)
- The damn mayor

She opened a drawer, revealing a folder labeled **"Leverage – Updated."** Inside were photos, videos, statements. All carefully categorized. All timestamped.

She picked up her Glock from its velvet-lined fruit bowl.

"Looks like it's time to fix this city."

End scene.

## The Spark

### POV: Nana May Jackson

The next morning in Dusty Springs smelled like rain-soaked pavement and old apologies. Clouds hung low like gossip ready to pour. The whole town buzzed—some from hangovers, some from Cinnamon's midnight "Healing the Wound He Gave You" TikTok Live, and a brave few still discussing the barbecue debacle like it was a historical event.

Nana May wasn't one for morning shows or social media, but she liked the sound of local scandal with her tea. It flavored the Earl Grey.

She stood in her kitchen, hands wrapped around a cracked "#1 Grandma (and She Will Hurt You)" mug, watching the local news on the tiny TV perched between her crockpot and an urn of expired whey protein she kept forgetting to throw out.

Onscreen, Mayor Carl DeWitt was sweating through his collar, stammering his way through a press conference held in front of a pothole so large a raccoon had recently applied for residency inside it.

"While we acknowledge that funds intended for pothole repair were—uh—reallocated," he said, voice wobbling, "we have initiated a strategic task force to reevaluate the disbursement of those resources through proper channels."

Translation: He'd spent that federal COVID money on his brother's vape shop and an air-conditioned gazebo outside city hall.

Nana didn't curse. Not aloud. But her teeth clenched like they had something unholy caught between them.

"That man got a GED in gibberish," she muttered.

A knock came at the door. She opened it without looking. It was **Maybelle "Mayday" Carter**, her best friend and retired local history teacher turned town gossip historian.

"You see the news?" Maybelle asked, stepping inside with a Tupperware of lemon squares and a file folder labeled *Possible Campaign Dirt – Dusty Springs '17–'22.*

"I saw," Nana said.

"He spent thirty grand on a Bluetooth fountain."

"I saw."

"They say he funneled public health money into a food truck that sells overpriced pickles in mason jars."

"I saw," Nana repeated, quieter now. Her hands were steady, but her breath came sharper.

She set her tea down.

"Mayday," she said, "fetch my folder."

Maybelle's eyebrows shot up. "Your…?"

"My leverage folder."

"Color-coded one with the blackmail receipts?"

"Exactly."

Maybelle didn't ask questions. She moved like a woman trained in cold war secrets and PTA sabotage.

Nana moved to her kitchen table, cleared off the Sunday paper, and set her GED diploma front and center. She stared at it for a moment—faded, wrinkled, but damn well earned. The same way she planned to earn City Hall.

"You serious?" Maybelle asked, placing the folder down gently like it was a sacred object.

"As a heart attack in a Waffle House."

"You really fixin' to run for mayor?"

"I'm fixin' to clean house," Nana said. "And not with Pine-Sol. With power."

She opened the folder.

Inside:

- Photos of councilmen tied to her antique bedposts. She paused on one—a man whose daughter she'd given a ride home from school just last fall. A pang of something heavy, like regret, settled in her chest. Not for the discipline he'd earned, but for the ugly truth that the only way to make him listen was to hold his shame hostage. She closed her eyes for a beat, then hardened them. This was bigger than one man's dignity. She turned the page.

- Screenshots of emails with subject lines like *"Regarding the foot stuff — discreet payment?"*

- Copies of tax write-offs for imaginary charities

- A blurry video of Mayor DeWitt at a karaoke bar in a diaper singing "Pony"

She had been collecting dirt for years, not because she wanted to ruin anyone—but because power unchallenged gets lazy. And Dusty Springs was lazy.

They paved the rich neighborhoods. They cleaned the parks in the white zip codes. They gave scholarships to cousins of the school board. And they thought nobody would notice because they did it with smiles and ribbon-cutting selfies.

Nana noticed.

And now? Now she was tired of cleaning up after fools in private when she could just run the damn show.

She opened her ancient laptop. It whirred like it was filing for retirement. The desktop background was a photo of her late husband standing in front of their first house—back when things cost less and meant more.

She opened a browser window and typed:

"How to run for mayor without a PAC or patience"

Pop-ups appeared: local election board, an ad for custom bumper stickers, a BuzzFeed quiz asking "Which Powerful Woman Are You?"

She clicked it. Answered quickly. Got: *"You're Olivia Pope, but meaner."*

Nana smiled.

Maybelle leaned over. "You gonna tell Tyrone?"

Nana sipped her tea again.

"Not yet. Let him stew in Tierra's truth serum for a while."

"And Cinnamon?"

"She can keep burning sage. I'll be lighting fire under the city budget."

She typed "Print" and waited. Her ancient printer groaned like it needed therapy and a firmware update.

Out came a form: *Candidate Filing Application – City of Dusty Springs.*

Nana signed it with the same pen she once used to write PTA complaints that made teachers retire early.

Maybelle clapped once, slow.

"You really gonna do it."

"I'm not doin' this for glory," Nana said, standing up and sliding the application into a manila envelope. "I'm doin' this because I'm tired of men with microphones and no morals. I'm tired of dusty old boys' clubs pretending they invented order."

She picked up her Glock from the fruit bowl and tucked it gently into her handbag. Just in case.

"Besides," she added, "someone's gotta remind these fools what discipline looks like."

They walked out together, heading to the courthouse in silence, their heels echoing on the pavement like revolution.

**[End of Chapter 1.]**

# Chapter 2: Campaign Kickoff and the Bingo Incident

### Courthouse Chaos – Nana Files to Run

### POV: Nana May Jackson

The Dusty Springs Municipal Building was a beige brick tomb for ambition.

It was the kind of government office that still had a bowl of peppermint discs by the door and a poster explaining how to write a check. The lobby smelled like expired Lysol and lost dreams. Ceiling tiles hung loose like they were on unpaid leave, and the American flag in the corner drooped like it had been personally betrayed by every mayor who sat here in the last two decades.

Nana May Jackson stepped inside like she owned the building and had already started reorganizing it in her head. Maybelle trailed behind her, fanning herself with a voter registration form.

"Why is it always humid inside courthouses?" Maybelle whispered. "Ain't nobody here except dust and disappointment."

"Because corruption sweats," Nana replied.

The receptionist looked up. She was young, disinterested, and scrolling through Instagram with the detached soul of someone who'd already seen too much nonsense for a Tuesday. Her name tag read **Cherise**, but the look in her eyes said **Try Me**.

"Can I help you?" Cherise asked without looking up from her screen.

"I'm here to file my candidacy paperwork," Nana said, pulling a perfectly folded manila envelope from her handbag.

Cherise squinted. "For what?"

Nana smiled. "Mayor."

The girl blinked once. "Like… of Dusty Springs?"

"No, baby. I came to file for Queen of England, but they told me I needed to start local."

Maybelle let out a cough that was definitely a smothered laugh.

Cherise sighed and disappeared into the back. They waited exactly eleven seconds before the sound of muffled whispers started leaking through the door.

"She serious?"
"I think that's the lady from the Facebook group."
"No, girl—that's *Mistress Maybelline*."

Nana didn't flinch.

The door opened and out stepped a man in a clip-on tie, khaki pants, and a panic disorder. He was sweating profusely and holding a form like it might bite him.

His nameplate said **Mr. Harold Dinsmore, City Clerk**, but the way he looked at Nana said **client who never forgot her safe word**.

"Ms. Jackson," he croaked.

"Mr. Dinsmore," she said smoothly. "You're looking flushed. I trust your blood pressure's stabilized since last time?"

He fumbled the folder. "Yes, yes ma'am. I mean—Mist—I mean—ma'am."

She took the paperwork from him and signed it with deliberate grace. One looped capital letter after another, like she was writing an oath on the Constitution.

26

"I assume you'll process this today?" she asked.

"Absolutely."

"No 'delays' like with the zoning permit last year?"

His entire spine tried to leave his body. "No ma'am."

"I'd hate to make another... appointment."

He shook his head so fast his glasses nearly fell off.

Maybelle leaned in. "She has that effect."

Harold nodded so hard it looked like a confession. "Everything will be filed and posted by noon."

"Good," Nana said, handing the form back. "And Harold?"

"Yes, ma'am?"

"If my name's not printed properly on that ballot, I'll assume your home printer's been working again. Especially since I mailed you the ink."

"Yes, ma'am."

"And tell the mayor I said hello. And goodbye."

They turned and walked out, heels tapping with the precision of drumline snare rolls on the march to war.

As they passed the receptionist, Cherise looked up from her phone just long enough to offer a stunned blink.

Nana winked. "Vote early, sugar. Or I might remember that DUI you tried to bury last year."

Outside, the sun greeted them with the same heat and indifference as always.

"Well," Maybelle said, fanning herself again, "that's the most excitement this building's had since they replaced the vending machine and someone cried about it."

"You know what I've learned?" Nana said as they crossed the street toward her Buick. "They don't fear revolution until the person bringing it wears orthopedic shoes and keeps receipts."

Maybelle handed her a bumper sticker they'd designed that morning.

**NANA MAY FOR MAYOR**
*Fix the Streets. Expose the Cheats.*

"You sure about this?" Maybelle asked, serious now.

Nana popped the trunk and placed the first stack of flyers inside.

"I was sure the first time someone called me 'Miss Jackson' and flinched while doing it."

She looked back at City Hall.

"And baby, I *am* for real."

### Team Mayday Assembles

### POV: Maybelle "Mayday" Carter

Maybelle Carter was many things—a retired educator, a world-class lemon square architect, and a gossip connoisseur with a memory like the IRS. But today? Today she was assembling a team to help a dominatrix grandma take down a corrupt mayor using nothing but sass, secrets, and printable flyers.

She sipped her iced tea, adjusted her glasses, and looked over the neatly drawn flowchart on Nana May's dining room table.

"I call it 'Operation: Bless and Destroy,'" she said proudly.

Nana leaned in to inspect the chart. There were arrows, color codes, and a hand-drawn caricature of Mayor DeWitt with devil horns and sagging khakis.

"Why he got a receding hairline and a diaper?" Nana asked.

"Because truth," Maybelle said. "Also, I got bored waiting for Ronny."

On cue, the screen door banged open and in waltzed **Cousin Ronny**, wearing a Bluetooth headset, a satin bomber jacket, and confidence that had not been earned in decades.

"Ladies, the revolution has arrived," he announced, holding up a selfie stick like it was a microphone. "I just went viral with a remix of Nana's courthouse strut set to 'Back That Azz Up.'"

"You filmed me?" Nana asked.

"Of course. You're iconic, Auntie. You got walkin'-into-a-slap energy."

"Keep filming without permission and I'll show you walkin'-into-a-lawsuit energy."

Maybelle chuckled. "We need him, Nana. He knows how to make things trend. Even if most of what he trends is chaos."

"Exactly," Ronny said, already setting up a tripod in the corner. "I'm your media director, content king, and I got a green screen in my trunk. Let's get this woman a TikTok following so deep they call her *Nana the Savage Sage*."

"You high?" Nana asked.

"Only on the idea of justice."

From the hallway came the sound of a clumsy knock. The door opened and **Quita** strolled in with a foil tray in one hand and a glitter pen in the other.

29

"Sorry I'm late," she said. "I was makin' shrimp rotel and breakin' up with a guy I met on Hinge who turned out to be my cousin's baby daddy. Again."

"Was it the same cousin?" Maybelle asked without looking up.

"Don't start."

Quita placed the tray on the table and flopped into a chair. "You said we was organizing? I love organizing. I once ran a vision board night that ended in three pregnancies and a moon ritual."

"We're not doing *that* kind of organizing," Nana said. "We're running a campaign. I need event logistics, people herded, things printed, signs distributed."

Quita grinned. "I can do that. I got a clipboard, a whistle, and no moral compass when it comes to bribing volunteers with Kool-Aid and gift cards."

Nana paused. "That's disturbingly useful."

"Thank you."

Maybelle laid out the campaign roles:

- **Ronny**: Social media manager, campaign video producer, and chaos containment specialist

- **Quita**: Field operations, volunteer wrangler, and event hype

- **Sister Velma** (currently out getting her blood pressure checked): Church liaison, mole, and flyer distribution inside enemy congregations

- **Maybelle**: Press secretary, research lead, and designated eye-roller

"And me?" Nana asked, raising an eyebrow.

Maybelle smiled. "You're the storm."

Nana gave a nod. "Good. Then let's rain hell on City Hall."

Ronny clapped. "Say less. I already got a draft campaign slogan: 'Vote Nana or Get Nana'd.'"

"No," Maybelle said flatly.

"'Vote Nana—She's Got the Receipts.'"

"Closer."

"'Vote Nana: She'll Whip This Town Into Shape.'"

Everyone paused.

Nana smiled, slowly.

"Print that one."

Ronny fist-pumped. "It's happening."

Quita already had her phone out, texting her exes and posting "volunteer opportunities" on her Instagram story with the caption *"Free shirts + drama."*

Maybelle looked around the table at this mismatched crew of glorious lunatics and troublemakers and felt a flicker of real power. Not institutional. Not bureaucratic. **Grassroots, baby. The kind with calluses and tea bags.**

She tapped her pen against the lemon square tin and raised her voice.

"Okay y'all. Nana's campaign kickoff is Bingo Night. We need bodies, buttons, and a backup plan in case someone throws a shoe."

Ronny grinned. "We got this."

Quita pulled out her clipboard. "I already bribed Sister Edna with banana pudding to wear a Nana shirt."

Maybelle smiled. "Then let's get this woman elected."

Nana stood slowly, adjusted her housecoat, and looked out the window at the town she was about to flip on its corrupt little head.

"Time to remind these fools who raised this place... and who's about to raise hell in it."

## Bingo Night Massacre

**POV: Nana May Jackson**

Bingo Night at First Triumph Holiness Tabernacle was less a game and more a **blood sport for the sanctified**.

The fellowship hall was packed. Not just with folding chairs and synthetic punch, but with decades of *mild beef*, unresolved choir feuds, and passive-aggressive battles disguised as "fellowship." The walls were beige, the carpet maroon, and the air thick with perfume, mothballs, and barely concealed judgment.

Nana May Jackson walked in wearing a teal pantsuit that could stun a bishop. On her left, Maybelle adjusted her "NANA 2025" brooch like it was armor. On her right, Quita handed out flyers with glitter on one side and *receipts* on the other. Behind them, Cousin Ronny rolled in a speaker that was not requested, not needed, and already playing a chopped and screwed gospel remix.

"Turn it down," Nana whispered through clenched teeth.

"But the vibe—" Ronny started.

"*Now.*"

He turned it down.

The crowd clocked them instantly. A group of deacons stiffened like someone had just whispered "audit." A few church mothers narrowed their eyes over their reading glasses. Sister Velma, bless her undercover heart, was already posted up near the refreshments, texting Nana updates under the code name **"Ezekiel 3:12."**

*Ezekiel 3:12*: Gregor's cousin is here. Wearing lavender. Looking petty.
*Ezekiel 3:13*: Pastor's here too. Smiling fake. Talking about "prayer warriors."

Nana smiled sweetly. "Let them try."

The bingo caller was **Sister Mildred**, an old rival from the Usher Board whose only hobbies were pronouncing numbers with unnecessary attitude and pretending she didn't remember the time she slept with two brothers in the choir and blamed "a dream."

Nana sat down with her card and dabber, waiting.

Halfway through the second round, it happened.

"B-twelve!" Sister Mildred shouted.

And then: "Speaking of B-words, ain't it funny how some people just *decide* they wanna be in politics now? No credentials, no morals, just nerve."

The room rippled. Neck-swivels. Throat-clears. Quita dropped a lemon square.

Nana looked up slowly.

A man in lavender slacks stood near the back, arms crossed, smiling like he paid for this moment. **Councilman Gregor**

**Blanchfield's cousin—Jasper.** A petty little man who once got banned from Sunday School for cheating at Uno and has never emotionally recovered.

"She wanna fix potholes?" Jasper called out. "She couldn't even fix her own husband—he ran off to Biloxi with a praise dancer!"

Gasps.

Maybelle's fan snapped open like a guillotine.

Ronny reached for his phone. "We recordin' this or nah?"

"Let him finish," Nana said. Calm. Cold.

Jasper strutted forward, emboldened. "Y'all really wanna vote for someone who disciplines grown men in her basement and thinks an orthotic arch support counts as campaign strategy?"

Laughter. Some of it nervous.

Pastor Devon "D-Stacks" Moore stood up slowly from his chair. "Let's remain respectful," he said, adjusting his robe. "We all know Miss Jackson is... colorful. And we respect that. But some roles," he added, eyes fixed on Nana, "were not meant for every woman."

Nana set down her dabber. Her card was one away from a blackout. Not that it mattered now.

She stood up.

And silence followed.

"You wanna talk about roles?" she said, voice low but slicing. "Let's talk about roles."

She took one step forward. Her heels clicked like punctuation.

"You're a pastor, Devon. A man of the cloth. And yet last Friday, you were in a private Etsy group selling 'anointed booty oil' for thirty-nine ninety-nine with a 'Buy two, get delivered' special."

Laughter. Screams.

"And you—Jasper." She turned. "Still mad the only job you ever held down was being a mascot for Jiffy Lube and you got fired for mooning traffic."

Sister Velma dropped a meatball. The deacons shifted in their seats like judgment was catching up.

"And let's not forget who really ain't qualified to speak: people who've been living off their cousin's WIC card for six years and still ain't filed taxes since Obama left."

Quita whispered, "Murder."

"Let me say this," Nana said, stepping fully into the middle of the room. "I raised this community. I changed diapers of half y'all's babies and buried more good men than this city ever honored. And while you were snickering behind stained-glass windows and misusing tithes to buy Bluetooth headsets, I was building a war chest and collecting receipts."

She pointed at the bingo board. "You wanna call numbers? Fine. Let me call a few."

She pulled out a folded list.

"Item one: The Mayor diverted $14,000 meant for school lunches to fund a city golf retreat. Item two: Councilwoman Jeannie's nephew got hired to fix potholes—he filled one with crushed Takis and a Bible verse."

Now full chaos.

"Bingo," Nana said.

Sister Mildred looked up, blinking. "You ain't got bingo."

"Oh, I got more than that," Nana replied.

She picked up a bingo ball, walked over to Jasper, and **gently tossed it into his lap**.

"Here's your number, baby. Try playing with dignity next time."

Ronny screamed. *"We are LIVE!"*

Phones came out. Twitter began vibrating. TikTok started looping the moment like it was the Zapruder film of Southern drama.

The video's caption read:
**"Granny Just Bodybagged the Bingo Hall #BingoBackhand #NanaForMayor #OrthopedicVengeance"**

Nana sat back down, smooth and unfazed. She looked at her card.

"Still one away," she murmured. "Figures."


**Pastor D-Stacks' Sermon Smackdown**

**POV: Pastor Devon "D-Stacks" Moore**

First Triumph Holiness Tabernacle was full to the fire code limit that Sunday.

People came early, pretending to be holy, but really just hoping for a second act of last night's Bingo Night Massacre. The fellowship hall had never recovered from the spiritual aftershocks of Nana May Jackson's bingo ball body slam. Every folding chair in the sanctuary was filled. Deacons were side-eying the youth choir. Ushers had doubled up on mints and extra fans. Even the old stained-glass Jesus seemed to be side-eyeing the altar with anticipation.

At 10:57 a.m., Pastor Devon Moore—known behind closed doors (and Etsy accounts) as **D-Stacks**—stood in the pulpit, bathed in light and delusion.

He wore a custom-tailored robe lined in gold trim and discreetly embroidered with his initials. His Bible was bookmarked with business cards for his LLC. The congregation fell silent as he spread his arms like he was about to summon thunder—or a camera crew.

He wasn't nervous, not exactly. He was a man of God. But God didn't have a TikTok account, and *Nana May sure as hell did now.*

"Saints," he began, with the practiced rhythm of a man who knew exactly how long to pause for dramatic effect, "today I come not just to preach, but to protect."

The murmurs began. He leaned in.

"There are wolves in pearls, family. Wolves in pearls."

A gasp somewhere in the back. Someone whispered, "He ain't talking about who I *think* he talking about…"

Pastor Moore adjusted his mic.

"We live in a time where *grandmothers* believe leadership is a matter of gossip and sass, not scripture and service. Where *dominant personalities* confuse control with calling."

He was good. Smooth. Polished. Smiling just enough to imply humility without ever touching it.

"Dusty Springs doesn't need flashy rebellion. It needs quiet obedience. It needs order. It needs God."

He looked over the congregation, letting his words marinate like a sermonized stew. But in the back pew, sitting with her arms crossed and her purse open just wide enough to show a glint of silver inside, sat **Nana May Jackson**—unbothered and unblinking.

She wore a matching hat and gloves. Her expression was mild, grandmotherly even. But her eyes? They glinted like someone who already had tomorrow's headlines scheduled.

Pastor Moore locked eyes with her for a second too long.

He continued.

"We must be vigilant against *counterfeit leaders*. Against self-appointed prophets of pettiness."

He didn't say her name. Didn't have to.

"She may entertain with words, but does she shepherd souls?"

Nana smiled. Tilted her head. Pulled out a pen and began writing something on a notepad labeled *"Sunday Receipts."*

Pastor Moore's smile twitched.

He turned the page in his Bible. "As it is written in Matthew 7:15, 'Beware of false prophets who come to you in sheep's clothing, but inwardly are ravenous wolves.'"

The congregation nodded, stirred.

"She ain't no sheep," whispered Deacon Al.

"She got a switchblade in her support hose," added someone else.

Pastor Moore raised his voice. "Some of y'all clapped for a woman who came into the Lord's house and used a *bingo ball* like a weapon. That's not strength—that's *spectacle.*"

Nana scribbled something. Quietly. Slowly.

Pastor Moore swallowed.

"But God," he said louder, "will not be mocked. And His church is not a platform for performance. It is a sanctuary of *humility.* Of *grace.* Of *order.*"

The choir behind him nodded, but with decreasing enthusiasm.

He was sweating now. Just a little. Underneath it all, there was a pinch of fear. Because he knew—**knew**—that Nana May had *footage.* Not rumors. Not gossip. Footage.

And if that went public?

Well, not even his "anointed essential oil blends" would be enough to save his seat.

He closed his Bible and stepped back from the mic. "Let us pray," he said. "Let us pray for discernment. For wisdom. And for the strength to reject chaos dressed as change."

The prayer was long, dramatic, and full of righteous innuendo.

When the organ swelled and the closing hymn began, Nana stood from the back pew. She nodded once at Maybelle, who mouthed, "That was a weak word."

As Nana passed by Pastor Moore on the way out, she paused. Just long enough for him to feel the gravity of her presence.

She leaned in and said, almost sweetly, "You use the pulpit like a stage. Shame you never learned how to close the curtain."

Then she walked out, hips swaying, purse swinging, victory already laced into her orthopedic stride.

Pastor Moore stood frozen behind the mic, hands clasped, praying not to God—but to Nana's restraint.

### The First Interview – Ronny Goes Rogue

**POV: Cousin Ronny**

Cousin Ronny had been waiting for this moment since 2003.

Back when he still believed his mixtape *"Bless the Streets, Vol. 1"* was going to change the culture and his Nokia flip phone could record high-quality freestyles in a parked Ford Taurus.

Now, in 2025, redemption had arrived—not through rap, not through SoundCloud, but through his legendary aunt Nana May Jackson and the campaign of the century.

His living room was transformed into what he called "**The Situation Studio**," which was really just:

- A wrinkled green screen tacked to the wall with thumbtacks and hope,

- A borrowed ring light from Quita (with one setting: *aggressive glare*),

- And a repurposed ironing board stacked with two iPhones, one webcam, and a lava lamp he insisted added "vibe frequency."

Nana sat in a padded folding chair in front of the green screen, wearing a blazer that didn't match her skirt on purpose and glasses she didn't need, but said "serious." She looked like the kind of woman who would run for office and *also* write your teacher a three-page letter when you got suspended.

Ronny adjusted his Bluetooth headset even though no one was calling him and cleared his throat like he was about to anchor CNN.

"Alright, Auntie," he said, hitting the livestream button. "We live in five, four, three—"

"We live now," said the phone, already broadcasting.

"—we live now," he corrected smoothly. "Dusty Springs, what's good! You already know who it is—Cousin Ronny, your neighborhood media mogul-slash-creative consultant—and today we got the future mayor of this dusty-ass town right here in my home studio. Say hello to the people, Nana."

Nana looked at the camera like she was trying to figure out where to direct disappointment.

"Hello, Dusty Springs. I'm Nana May Jackson, and I'm running for mayor to clean up this town—ethically, financially, and if necessary, with Lysol and a belt."

Ronny slapped his knee. "That's what I'm talkin' about!"

He jumped up, spun the camera too fast, then adjusted it back. The image flickered, briefly showing a poster of Tupac next to a photo of Nana holding a casserole at a funeral.

"So, Nana," Ronny said, repositioning the mic like a podcast pro, "what inspired you to run? Was it the potholes, the pandemic mismanagement, or just the general spiritual mustiness of City Hall?"

Nana folded her hands. "All of the above. Plus, I'm tired of watching people get elected because they got a cousin on the board and a secret OnlyFans. This town needs discipline. And not the kind I offer in private."

Ronny's eyes went wide. "Wait, are we talkin' about the—"

"Ronny."

"Right. Respect. Redacted."

He glanced at the laptop screen. The comments were flying.

*"Who is this lady???"*
*"I'm voting for her and I don't even live there."*
*"Wait—did she say 'OnlyFans'??"*
*"HOT!"*
*"Where do I buy merch???"*

"You're trending already," Ronny said. "I ain't even dropped the campaign anthem yet."

"Don't drop anything unless it's voter registration cards," Nana said.

He laughed nervously and flipped to his *next question index cards*—a stack of wrinkled Post-its held together with a rubber band and faith.

"Alright, now let's talk about your platform," he said. "What's priority number one?"

"Priority number one," Nana said calmly, "is cleaning up the mess. Misused funds. Dirty streets. Nepotism in the zoning committee. Also, removing that moldy vending machine in the DMV. It's been humming like it's possessed."

Ronny nodded, impressed. "So like… practical revolution."

"Precisely."

Then, because the devil has impeccable timing, Ronny's phone started vibrating with a notification from his **Google Drive** labeled *"Nana Secrets – Do Not Open During Livestream."*

He clicked it.

A folder popped open on-screen—visible to the audience for a split second before he minimized it—but it was too late. They'd seen it.

*Nana_May_Pressure_Points.pdf*
*Video_ChiefBeaumont_On_Leash.mp4*
*MayorKaraoke_GolfFundMisuse.mov*

The chat exploded.

*"NAHHH SHE GOT DIRT ON EVERYBODY"*
*"That's the chief of police in latex???"*
*"This is better than Real Housewives."*

Nana gave him a slow look. The kind that could break generational curses.

"Ronny."

"I didn't mean to click it—"

"You didn't *not* mean to."

She adjusted her blazer and looked directly into the camera.

"Well, I suppose since the cat's out the bag and walking in heels—yes, I've spent the last several years documenting Dusty Springs' political and moral rot. If that makes me a threat to the establishment... *good.*"

The room went dead silent. Then someone in the live chat posted:

*"I'd sell my auntie for a mayor like this."*

Ronny leaned forward. "Auntie… I mean, Madam Mayor… you just broke Dusty Springs internet."

Nana stood.

"I didn't come here to be famous," she said. "I came here to fix the town. But if the truth goes viral on the way? Then let it fly."

And with that, she picked up her purse, gave Ronny a look that promised mild violence and extreme pride, and walked out of frame.

The live ended.

The memes began.

**[End of Chapter 2.]**

# Chapter 3: Bless This Smoke: The Sage-Off Begins

**The Unholy Trinity**

**POV: Cinnamon Belle**

Setting: The back room of Pastor Ricky's Glory & Dominion Mega-Tabernacle, which looked less like a prayer room and more like a mob boss's lounge.

The leather was plush, the whiskey was top-shelf, and the ambition in the room was thick enough to bottle and sell as a fragrance. Cinnamon sat across from Pastor Ricky Walls and Barbara Cain, the two pillars of Dusty Springs' old guard. Pastor Ricky, a man whose suits cost more than a teacher's salary, smiled a predator's smile. Barbara, a real estate developer with a stare that could curdle holy water, tapped her perfectly manicured nails on the polished oak table.

"The Lord has laid a vision upon my heart," Pastor Ricky began, his voice smooth as aged bourbon. "And that vision, my dear Cinnamon, has your face on it."

Cinnamon preened, adjusting the lapels of her white blazer. "The ancestors have been speaking to me as well. They say it's time for a new energy in the mayor's office."

Barbara cut through the spiritual fluff with the precision of a diamond-tipped saw. "Let's be clear. Mayor DeWitt is out. He's not running. That leaves a power vacuum. Nana May Jackson is a sentimental folk hero, but she's a political amateur. You, on the other hand, have influence. You have a following. You're... malleable."

"I am a vessel," Cinnamon corrected, though she knew exactly what Barbara meant.

"Of course, you are," Pastor Ricky said, pouring her a small glass of amber liquid. "A vessel for change. A vessel for... progress. Barbara and I, along with our associates, are prepared to fund your campaign. We believe you represent the future of Dusty Springs."

The unspoken part hung in the air: a future we can control. They saw her as the perfect puppet—spiritual, popular, and with just enough ego to be easily manipulated. They needed a friendly face in City Hall to approve their zoning changes, overlook their tax-exempt statuses, and keep the town's pesky new progressives in check.

"Nana is a problem," Barbara stated flatly. "She's got the people's ear, and she's asking questions about budgets and permits. We need someone who can distract them with... what is it you call it? Vibrations?"

"Vibrational alignment," Cinnamon said, taking a delicate sip of the whiskey. It burned, but it tasted like power. "I can rally the youth. The spiritual. The ones who believe in healing over policy."

"Exactly," Pastor Ricky boomed, clapping his hands together. "You'll be the face of a new, enlightened Dusty Springs. We'll handle the strategy, the funding, the... less savory aspects of a campaign. All you have to do is what you do best: shine."

Cinnamon smiled, a slow, calculated spreading of her lips. They thought they were playing her. But she had her own agenda. Let them think she was their puppet. When she was in office, she would be the one pulling the strings.

"Then it's settled," she said, raising her glass. "To a new Dusty Springs. Healed, whole, and under new management."

They toasted. The unholy trinity was formed. The campaign had begun, not with a rally, but with a backroom deal sealed in whiskey and ambition.

## Scene 12: The Sage-Off at the Farmer's Market

### POV: Maybelle Carter

The Dusty Springs Farmer's Market used to smell like honeydew, kettle corn, and the vague disappointment of locally-sourced soap. But this morning, it smelled like judgment, burnt lavender, and a thousand years of weaponized yoga energy.

Maybelle Carter stood near the hand-churned butter stand, arms crossed, eyebrow lifted. Beside her, Quita held up her phone, filming live for *Nana Nation's* TikTok.

"You gettin' this?" Maybelle asked.

"Oh, I'm gettin' it," Quita said. "If this fool lights one more bundle of sage like it's Pentecost, I'm zoomin' in on the fire department's reaction."

Across the cobblestone square, a circle of women dressed in pastel linen and bad intentions stood swaying gently, rhythmically, like backup dancers for an unsolicited TED Talk. In the center stood **Cinnamon Belle**, ex-church soloist turned spiritual influencer, wearing a floor-length crocheted cape and a headwrap the size of a picnic table.

She was chanting.

Loudly.

"Cleanse this space of chaos... cleanse this town of trauma... cleanse our auras from... THE WHIP OF THE WICKED GRANDMOTHER!"

A few people clapped. One person sneezed. A small dog barked in confusion.

"She really called Nana a wicked grandmother?" Quita muttered.

"Loud enough for Jesus to file a complaint," Maybelle replied.

Cinnamon held up a bundle of sage the size of a toddler's forearm. The words "**NANA MAY JACKSON**" were written across it in red Sharpie.

"We release this energy," she declared, "this spirit of domination, deceit, and pearl-clutching tyranny!"

She lit the sage with a comically oversized matchstick— probably bought from Etsy or some fake voodoo-themed subscription box—and held it high. Smoke curled into the sky.

Someone in the crowd coughed dramatically. Another fan snapped open. An old man muttered, "Lord, y'all done turned Whole Foods into holy war."

Cinnamon began spinning slowly, smoke trailing behind her like she was summoning the ancestors of petty grievances past.

Maybelle narrowed her eyes. "She better not let that smoke touch my blouse. This silk was prayed over."

Quita smirked. "You want me to go out there and cause a *light* scene? Like… glitter-in-the-burn-bundle kind of light?"

"No. Not yet. Let her finish roasting herself first."

Cinnamon continued. "And may the spirit of the matriarch in *chains* be bound in holy thread, that she may not tempt this town with her sinister straps of seduction!"

Gasps.

"Did she just say—?" Quita blinked. "She talkin' 'bout Nana's *side hustle*?"

"Oh, she going there," Maybelle said, unfolding her sunglasses. "Good. Now I don't have to pretend to be diplomatic later."

Cinnamon struck a pose, breathing deeply like the crowd was about to erupt into applause.

They didn't.

A baby cried. A vendor dropped a peach. Someone's Bluetooth speaker nearby blared an accidental ringtone: "Back That Azz Up."

Then, in the calm after the chaos, **a voice sliced through the silence**:

"Now that y'all done gentrified incense…"

Heads turned.

There, at the edge of the circle, stood **Nana May Jackson**.

Black dress. Wide-brimmed hat. Cane in one hand. A Kroger bag in the other. Expression: Sunday School teacher who just caught you smoking behind the church van.

Cinnamon froze.

"Oh no," Quita whispered. "She done materialized like Candyman."

Nana stepped forward.

"I came for plums," she said, holding up the Kroger bag. "But instead I find y'all out here playing Hogwarts in Jesus' name."

Laughter. Soft at first. Nervous. But it grew.

Cinnamon regained her composure. "We're cleansing, Nana. Something you clearly don't believe in. You walk around with dark energy wrapped in Spanx."

Nana smiled politely.

"Sweetheart, I *invented* dark energy. I bathed in it before brunch."

Cinnamon raised her voice. "You're manipulating this town with fear, dominance, and barely concealed threats."

"And you're manipulating 'em with crystals and Amazon wishlists. Let's not pretend one hustle's holier than the other."

Murmurs.

Cinnamon turned to the crowd. "She's not a leader. She's a *punishment in pearls!* A disciplinary demon!"

Nana stepped into the center of the circle.

"Better a demon who gets things done than an angel who can't organize a bake sale without a chakra chart."

Cinnamon tried to respond. But then Nana pulled out a small vial of oil, kissed it, and poured a drop on the pavement.

"What's that?" Cinnamon asked.

"Blessing oil," Nana said. "Got it from my grandma's kitchen. It's half holy water, half Crisco, and a splash of something only the *old folks* know about."

"What's it for?"

Nana looked her dead in the eye.

"For sticking around. After the smoke clears."

And then she left. Just like that.

No mic drop. No punchline. Just vibes and vengeance.

The farmer's market didn't erupt in cheers.

It *simmered*.

People looked around at each other, unsure what just happened—but knowing deep in their spirit that **Nana May had just won the sage-off without lighting a damn thing.**

Cinnamon stood in the middle of her smoke circle, uncertain. Her bundle fizzled in her hand like a dying dream. Someone in the crowd coughed again.

Then Maybelle leaned over to Quita and whispered, "Time to make flyers."


## Cinnamon Belle's Confessional Livestream

### POV: Cinnamon Belle

Cinnamon Belle hadn't slept.
She hadn't saged.
She hadn't even exfoliated—and for a woman whose skincare regimen involved nine steps and two ancestor prayers, that was near-apocalyptic.

She was in crisis.

The Farmer's Market debacle had already gone viral on *TikTok*, *Black Twitter*, *Christian Facebook*, and—God help her—even *Nextdoor*, where a woman named Janet had asked, "Is this witchcraft or a craft fair?" and got 146 upvotes.

She paced her bedroom, ring light flickering like a divine interrogation beam.

Behind her: a wall of inspirational quotes on peel-and-stick decals ("She is Clothed in Dignity & Discount Codes") and a tapestry of a lioness wearing a crown, purchased after her third chakra cleanse.

She fixed the camera. Took a breath.

And went *live*.

"Peace, family..." she began, voice trembling. "Peace and abundant clarity in this difficult, chaotic time."

Her nose was shiny. Her contour was off. The filter was set to **"Woodland Sparkle"**, which she didn't realize until two minutes in when someone commented:

*"Why this woman got raccoon ears on while confessing??"*

Still, she pressed on.

"I never thought I'd be attacked for spreading *healing.* I never imagined I'd be *persecuted* for loving my community through sage and seasonal produce."

Another comment popped up:

*"Girl no one persecuted you, she just out-spiritualed you in orthopedic shoes."*

Cinnamon blinked. Tears welled up. Whether emotional or allergy-induced, no one could say.

"Y'all don't see what I see. This... this woman, Nana May Jackson, is not who she claims to be. She may appear wise, but that is *Lucifer's oldest trick!*"

The comment section ignited.

*"Not you comparing Nana to Satan while lookin' like Lisa Frank's leftover bookmark."*

*"Say what you want, Nana got more receipts than CVS."*
*"Did you cry before or after you saw the views?"*

Cinnamon sniffed. Snatched a tissue.

"I'm being targeted. I've received… threatening emails. Spam from Hotmail. One man sent me a picture of a sandwich and said 'you're toast.'"

She held up her phone.

"And if anything happens to me, y'all will know…
the **Dominatrix of Dusty Springs** did it."

That was a mistake.

The chat *exploded.*

*"Dominatrix of Dusty Springs is the title of her memoir now."*
*"Where do I preorder tho??"*
*"You jealous she makin' moves in heels and you spiralin' in sage smoke."*

Cinnamon's eyes widened. "This is harassment. Cyber-harassment. I'm a spiritual leader!"

The raccoon ears shimmered softly on her face.

A pause. Then she whispered, "My journey started when I saw God's face in an avocado pit—"

Cut to black.

She'd accidentally hit the "End Stream" button with her elbow.

A beat of silence.

She stared at the blank screen.

"No," she whispered. "No no no—"

Her phone buzzed.

**New Notification:** *You've been tagged in 47 new memes.*

Another:

**Trending Hashtag:**
#RaccoonReckoning
#NotMyHealer
#ClothedInInsecurityAndInconsistency

She turned slowly. Her cat, Sage-Marie, blinked at her in judgment.

Cinnamon Belle sat back on her throw pillow throne, mascara smudging, ring light dimming.

"This town is evil," she whispered.

Meanwhile, three blocks away, Nana May was sipping decaf tea and watching the replay with one eyebrow raised and a notepad labeled:

**"Unfit Opponent: Breakdown Catalog"**
☑ Sage Bundle Overload
☑ Crocodile Tears
☑ Digital Collapse
☑ Avocado Prophecy

She chuckled once, sharp and low.

Then circled the last line and wrote beneath it:
**"Stage 3: Silence Her With Style."**


**Sister Velma's Deep Intel Dump**

**POV: Sister Velma Green**

Sister Velma Green didn't look like a spy.
She looked like she judged your potato salad and hid

peppermints in every coat pocket she owned.

She looked like she could kill you with silence—and probably had.

Which made her the **perfect** mole.

She arrived at the "Healing and Harmony Circle" event wearing a lavender windbreaker and a smile that had *just enough* confusion to make her blend in with the other ladies pretending to know what "divine alignment aromatherapy" meant.

The park smelled like sage, fermented goji berries, and denial. Folding chairs circled a speaker's podium made from repurposed bamboo and arrogance.

Cinnamon Belle stood at the front, addressing the crowd like she was launching a cult franchise.

"Welcome, radiant souls," she said, hands open like a flight attendant for narcissism. "Let us now center our breath and release the trauma of public shame and inappropriate elders."

Velma sat near the back, beside a woman named Charlene who wore a crystal on her forehead and shoes made of recycled kombucha labels.

"First time?" Charlene asked.

Velma nodded. "Heard this helps with blood pressure and the urge to slap people."

Charlene hummed approvingly.

Velma tapped her brooch once.

A **tiny green light blinked** beneath the rhinestones.

She was live.

The camera—hidden inside a thrift-store special from the "Church Auntie Accessories" collection—began recording everything.

Cinnamon continued.

"We are not just resisting corruption. We are creating frequency harmony. We are aligning Dusty Springs with the divine feminine."

Velma leaned to the side. Whispered into her purse, "Y'all hear this?"

The voice recorder inside picked it up. She tapped her hearing aid. Audio sync confirmed.

Then she did what every good infiltrator does.

She listened.

And listened.

And took notes.


**What She Uncovered:**

**1. The Healing Circle was backed by The Men's Civic Club.**
A shadowy group of old-school politicians and failed Elks Lodge members trying to reestablish control of city politics with Cinnamon as the smiling, sage-burning puppet.

**2. The funding trail was dirty.**
Velma slipped into the folding-chair perimeter after the event and caught a man in a $600 sweatsuit (unironically labeled "conscious wealth") handing Cinnamon an envelope.

She zoomed in. Got a shot. It contained:

- Cash

- Business cards
- A flyer for "Cinnamon Belle's Holy Hustle Multi-Level Marketing Opportunity"

### 3. Cinnamon was building a donor list under the guise of a "Sound Bath Healing Ceremony."

Translation: if you showed up to sit in a circle and listen to ocean noises through a Bluetooth speaker, you were added to a targeted email campaign with donation buttons labeled "Reclaim Our Town."

Velma pretended to be sleepy, snored once, and used the opportunity to snag a sign-in sheet.

### 4. There were *fake petition signatures* collected at the event.

Supposedly to "declare Dusty Springs a spiritual sanctuary"— but the fine print allowed the city council to push a resolution disqualifying "morally compromised candidates."

Guess whose name was highlighted in Sharpie next to "moral compromise"?

That's right: **Nana May Jackson**.

Velma took photos.

Then took a muffin.

Then took her leave.


### Soft Witchery:

She returned home and opened up her dropbox folder titled **"Exposing Soft Witchery – Evidence Batch."**
She uploaded:

- 3 full HD videos
- 2 incriminating audio clips
- 1 photo of Cinnamon's campaign aide snorting cayenne powder for "energy alignment"
- The complete sign-in sheet with donor targets circled in red

She called Maybelle.

"Say it," Maybelle answered. "I know you been dyin' to say it."

Velma grinned.

"The sage ain't the only thing that got smoked today."


## Nana's Counterstrike Sermon at The People's Pit BBQ

### POV: Nana May Jackson

The People's Pit BBQ wasn't known for politics.
It was known for its brisket, its homemade sweet tea that could put a diabetic in a coma, and its owner, DeShawn "D-Bone" Jefferson, who ran the place like a meat-slinging philosopher.

But today, it became the church, the courtroom, and the battlefield.

Nana May Jackson stood behind a fold-out podium that had once held sauce samples and was now covered in a lace tablecloth and framed voter registration forms. Behind her, a red, white, and mustard-yellow banner read:

**"Let the Spirit Move You (Toward the Ballot Box)."**

The Pit was packed.
Locals fanned themselves with napkins.

Teens snuck ribs under folding chairs.
The mayor's assistant was parked across the street pretending to read a book but clearly recording.

Nana adjusted her glasses and leaned into the microphone.

"Good evening, Dusty Springs."

The crowd answered in that Southern half-mumble of recognition.

"I didn't call y'all here today to talk about politics," she said. "I called y'all here to talk about **smoke.**"

Someone in the back coughed in approval.

"Now I know there's been a lotta it lately—sage smoke, rumor smoke, digital smoke, and that one time Cinnamon Belle nearly set a zucchini stand on fire at the Farmer's Market."

Laughter rippled through the crowd.

"But let's be clear," she said, voice rising, "smoke without heat don't cook nothin'. And smoke without truth just chokes the air."

Amen.

Nana stepped around the podium.

"I've been called a lot of things this week. Jezebel. Dommy Mommy. Weaponized Elder. Bless your hearts, by the way. Took creativity. But let me be the one to tell you who I *am.*"

She pointed to herself, softly.

"I'm a grandmother.
I'm a fighter.
I'm a woman who's seen this town turn on its own while pretending to pray for 'em in public.
I'm the woman who wiped noses, paid library fines, marched

59

when it was scary, and still shows up to city council meetings even when they 'accidentally' turn off my mic."

A pause. Heavy. Honorable.

"I ain't here to be your influencer. I ain't got no filter packs or detox teas. I drink real tea—with sugar—and I read real books with real history that some folks round here want erased."

Cheers. A few people stood.

"And I know," she said, holding her arms out, "that I ain't perfect. Lord knows I got side hustles. Some of y'all paid me for 'em."

Laughter *and* applause.

"But what I ain't never done is lie to you. Not once. Not for money. Not for votes. Not for vanity."

The crowd went quiet, respectful. Listening now with their whole spirit.

"Now Miss Belle," she continued, not naming her fully but everyone knew, "she wants to cleanse the town with rose water and ring lights. But I ask you: who fed you when the power was out? Who got Miss Ruby's porch fixed after the hurricane when the city claimed there was no funding?"

Hands shot up.

"Who helped y'all grandkids register for community college? Who calls the coroner's office when y'all pastors get caught in the strip club and try to fake their deaths again?"

Shouts. Laughter. One hallelujah.

Nana nodded.

"That's right. *I did.* Not for clout. Not for claps. But because it was *right.*"

She walked down from the podium and picked up a small bundle from a basket on the ground.

"This here's lavender and peppermint from my garden," she said, holding it high. "I didn't burn it to erase nobody. I'm giving it away. Why? Because healing ain't about burning bridges. It's about building tables—and makin' sure folks got a seat and a damn plate."

She handed it to a teenage girl in the front row who looked one TikTok away from apathy. The girl blinked and held it like a relic.

Nana turned back.

"We can't fix this town with fake peace and influencer tears. We fix it with honesty. With backbone. With community."

She smiled.

"And with ribs."

A pitmaster lifted a pan of brisket and the crowd *lost it*.

Applause. Cheers. Somebody started a chant:

**"NANA! NANA! NANA!"**

She raised a hand, humbly.

"Now y'all grab a plate, sign that voter form, and tell Cinnamon I said… bless her misunderstood heart."

The mic cut. The grill flared. The smell of smoked meat and revolution filled the air.

Nana May Jackson had just baptized her campaign in hickory and holy fire.


**The Flyers War and Political Billboard Vandalism**

## POV: Cousin Ronny "Razor" Jackson

Cousin Ronny Jackson never meant to be a political operative. He just owned a barbershop, ran a mildly viral meme page, and once duct-taped an iPad to a drone for better protest footage. But this week? He'd become the Banksy of Dusty Springs.

It started with the flyers.

Monday morning, folks woke up to Cinnamon Belle's face plastered on every available surface—utility poles, stop signs, church bulletins, even the side of a Shoney's delivery truck. Each flyer was professionally printed and aggressively beige, featuring Cinnamon doing a soft-focus pose like she was auditioning for a gospel-themed romcom.

### Text:

*"Cinnamon Belle: Heal the Town. Save the Soul. Cancel the Chaos."*

Underneath, a Bible quote taken wildly out of context and what looked like a QR code linked to an MLM.

Ronny peeled one off a pole. Squinted.

"Why she look like she smellin' a lie?" he muttered.

He tossed it in the trash.

Then he got to work.


### By Tuesday, new flyers hit the streets.

Nana May's face—stoic, fierce, and wearing her signature pearls—was Photoshopped onto Beyoncé's *Lemonade* album cover. In the background: flames, voting booths, and Cinnamon Belle chasing her own wig in the wind.

**Text:**

*"Don't Sage It—Save It. Vote Nana May Jackson: Mayor, Matriarch, Mayhem Manager."*

Another version showed Nana with her cane pointed like a staff, standing over a CGI demon labeled "Negligent Infrastructure."

By Wednesday, the flyer war had escalated to digital.

Ronny's meme account, **@BarberianLogic**, released a series called *"Who's Your Mayor?"*

- Cinnamon Belle, labeled: "Filter Queen, Funded by Flakes."

- Nana May, labeled: "Bakes cornbread, buries corruption."

Hashtag: **#PearlsNotProps**

Then came the *Billboard Incident.*


**There was a billboard just off Route 6.**
For years it advertised local lawyers and sometimes used car sales.
This week, it had a smiling picture of Cinnamon Belle in a pink power suit, arms open like she was about to baptize a zoning committee.

**Original Text:**

*"Vote Belle. Because We Need Healing."*

**Revised Text (Thursday morning):**

*"Vote Belle. Because We Need Help."*

Underneath, in red spray paint:

**"Holy Ho vs. Dommy Mom — Pick Your Fighter."**

Ronny heard about it while giving a teenager a high-top fade. His phone buzzed with a text from Quita:

**"You did this, didn't you?"**

He replied with a gif of Kermit sipping tea and a peach emoji.

**By Friday, the billboard had made the local news.**

News anchor Sharlene Mims stood in front of it, visibly flustered.

"This billboard was defaced late last night," she said, gesturing toward the text. "Police say there is no suspect—though online forums suggest a local social media influencer known as 'Barberian Logic' may have information."

Cut to Ronny, standing in his barbershop, surrounded by framed photos of Malcolm X, Tupac, and Nana May holding a pie.

He smiled.

"All I know," he told the camera, "is that Dusty Springs is finally payin' attention."

**Nana May walked in later that afternoon.**

"Ronny," she said without looking up from her purse, "I said *flyers*, not *graffiti*."

"Technically, it's political satire," he said, lining up a client's beard.

She raised an eyebrow.

"And I may or may not have a stencil of Cinnamon Belle's quote-face now," he added.

Nana sighed. "Just make sure she don't sue."

"She'd have to prove she's got a brand worth suing *for* first."

Nana allowed the corner of her mouth to twitch—just once.

"Also," Ronny continued, "the memes are out of control. Someone made a Mortal Kombat poster with you and Cinnamon. Your special move is called 'Receipt Slam.' Hers is 'Passive-Aggressive Aura Bomb.'"

"Let the people laugh," Nana said. "But when they vote, they better *remember who fed them.*"

Ronny nodded. "Already printed on the new bumper stickers."

**"Vote Nana: She'll Feed You, Read You, and Bury You (in Respect)."**

Nana smiled.

"And that's why I keep you around."


**[End of Chapter 3.]**

# Chapter 4: Scandals, Sermons, and Strapbacks

## The Senior Center Coup

**POV: Cinnamon Belle**

**Setting: Dusty Springs Senior Living Center - Community Room**

Nana's campaign saw the Senior Living Center as a guaranteed win. It was her home turf, filled with people she'd known for decades. Her team had planned a simple "Meet and Greet" with weak lemonade and stories from the good old days. They got complacent. They didn't see Cinnamon coming.

Cinnamon didn't arrive with sage and crystals. She came with an army of volunteers, a U-Haul full of donated goods, and a meticulously organized plan. While Nana's team was still setting up a single folding table, Cinnamon's crew was executing a full-scale charm offensive. They transformed the drab community room into a vibrant, welcoming space with comfortable new chairs, warm blankets for every resident, and a "Tech Help" station where smiling young volunteers patiently fixed residents' phones and set up video calls with their grandchildren.

But the masterstroke was the food. Instead of sad, store-bought cookies, Cinnamon had partnered with "Thelma's Kitchen," a beloved local soul food restaurant, to provide a full, hot lunch. The smell of fried chicken, collard greens, and macaroni and cheese filled the halls, drawing residents out of their rooms like a siren song.

When Nana and Maybelle finally arrived, they walked into a full-blown Cinnamon Belle love fest. The room was buzzing.

Residents were eating, laughing, and being genuinely cared for. Cinnamon was moving through the room, not as a mystical guru, but as a competent and compassionate organizer. She wasn't talking about chakras; she was talking about improving their Medicare Advantage plans, funding better wheelchair-accessible transportation, and organizing weekly social events.

Maybelle was aghast. "She stole our event and made it better."

Nana watched, her expression unreadable, as Cinnamon knelt beside the wheelchair of an elderly man, Mr. Henderson, and helped him figure out his new tablet. He looked up at Cinnamon with pure gratitude. "No one's ever taken the time to show me this," he said, his voice thick with emotion. "They just assume we're too old to learn."

"Nonsense," Cinnamon said warmly, her voice captured by the local news cameras her team had conveniently tipped off. "It's my pleasure, sir. Our elders deserve respect and resources, not just on voting day, but every day."

The soundbite was perfect. The visuals were even better.

Later that evening, Nana's campaign war room was silent as they watched the fallout online. Ronny scrolled through the "Dusty Springs Community Forum" on Facebook.

"It's a bloodbath, Auntie," he said grimly. A comment from a user named 'Gladys_P_72' read: "Nana's folks offered me a pamphlet. Cinnamon's team fixed my iPad and fed me the best fried chicken I've had since 1998. My vote ain't confused." Another post, with a picture of Cinnamon hugging a resident, had over 500 likes: "This is what leadership looks like. Not just talk, but action. #BelleCares"

The headline on the local news blog was devastating: "Belle's 'Senior Solidarity' Event Outshines Jackson's Old-School Approach, Raises Questions About Campaign's Connection to Voters."

For the first time, Nana's team was on the defensive. They had been outmaneuvered, out-organized, and out-classed. Cinnamon had won the day not with spiritual platitudes, but with tangible acts of service. She had proven she could be more than just a caricature, and in doing so, she won a crucial demographic Nana had taken for granted. The race was no longer a landslide; it was a fight.

## The Backfire in the Blogosphere

**POV: Mixed**

Setting: Barbara Cain's office, then the internet.

Fresh off the triumph of the "Senior Center Coup," Cinnamon's campaign was riding a wave of positive press for the first time. Her backers, Barbara Cain and Pastor Ricky, decided it was the perfect moment to press their advantage and go for the jugular. They would use this newfound goodwill as cover for a brutal, personal attack designed to permanently frame Nana as a deviant, a hypocrite, and unfit for public office.

They convened in Barbara Cain's opulent, sterile office for a war council. Cinnamon was patched in on a large screen, looking radiant and confident.

"The senior event was a masterstroke, my dear," Barbara said, a rare note of approval in her voice. "You've shown you can be more than just... incense and intentions. Now, while the town is seeing you as the compassionate choice, we strike."

68

"The iron is hot," Pastor Ricky agreed, steepling his fingers. "It is time to reveal the... moral rot at the core of the Jackson campaign. It is time to talk about her so-called 'side hustle'."

Barbara smirked. "I've already made the call. The Dusty Dish is preparing a feature. We'll paint her not as a community matriarch, but as the 'Mistress of Mayhem,' a shadowy figure who uses her 'skills of seduction and submission' to control the town's elite."

"We can use the photos we found," Pastor Ricky added. "The blurry ones of her in that leather outfit. We'll call it her 'dungeon uniform'."

Cinnamon shifted uncomfortably on screen. "Are we sure about this? The last few attacks haven't exactly landed."

"This is different," Barbara insisted, her voice sharp. "This isn't about sage or flyers. This is about sin. This is about shaming her in front of the church-going folks who form her base. We will also weave in the narrative about her grandson, Tyrone. We'll frame him as her 'financially compromised enforcer,' a 'bagman for her backroom deals,' using his money troubles as proof that he's on her illicit payroll."

"It's a two-pronged attack," Pastor Ricky summarized with satisfaction. "She's a sexual deviant, and her family is corrupt. It will shatter her image as a righteous grandmother."

Cinnamon, buoyed by her recent success and the persuasive confidence of her backers, finally nodded. "Alright. Let's do it."

The attack dropped the next morning. The headline on "The Dusty Dish" was a masterpiece of pearl-clutching outrage: EXCLUSIVE: MAYORAL HOPEFUL NANA JACKSON'S SECRET LIFE OF SIN! INSIDE THE 'DUNGEON OF

DISCIPLINE' AND THE GRANDSON WHO DOES HER DIRTY WORK!

For about an hour, it worked. The comments section filled with shocked emojis and whispers. But then, something shifted. The narrative didn't just flip; it did a full-blown acrobatic back handspring with a perfect landing.

In Nana's campaign headquarters (her living room), Quita and Ronny stared at the screen, not in horror, but in a state of stunned, joyous disbelief.

"They… they really thought this would work?" Quita asked, a slow, wicked grin spreading across her face.

Ronny was already typing, his fingers flying across the keyboard like he was composing a symphony of petty. "Work? Honey, they just handed us our entire marketing strategy on a silver platter of stupidity."

The Dusty Springs Community Forum exploded, but not with outrage. With glee.

Commenter 1: "Wait, so Nana is a powerful, self-made businesswoman who holds powerful men accountable AND she's running for mayor? Where do I donate AGAIN?"

Commenter 2: "A dominatrix, you say? So she knows how to handle people who don't listen and how to manage a budget. SIGN ME UP."

Commenter 3: "They tried to shame her with a side hustle and instead they gave her a superpower. LMAO."

Commenter 4: "So all those corrupt politicians were her clients? This woman has been cleaning up the town for YEARS. She's got my vote."

Within the hour, Ronny had launched a new line of campaign merchandise that sold out in minutes. T-shirts that read:

"NANA MAY JACKSON: WHIPPING THE CITY INTO SHAPE."

Bumper stickers with: "My Safe Word is Transparency."

And a new campaign poster featuring a stylized silhouette of Nana holding a gavel in one hand and a whip in the other. The tagline: "Discipline. Decency. Deliverance."

The hashtag #DominatrixMayor started trending locally, then regionally. The story, meant to be a scandal, had been instantly reframed as a testament to Nana's power, her fearlessness, and her refusal to be shamed. It was the most successful fundraising day of her campaign.


Back in her kitchen, Maybelle showed Nana the new merchandise designs on her tablet. Nana squinted at a T-shirt that read, "The Dungeon Elected the Queen."

She took a long, slow sip of her sweet tea, a thoughtful expression on her face.

"Well," she said finally, a small, dangerous smile playing on her lips. "Tell Ronny to make sure the T-shirts are 100% cotton. If we're gonna be ratchet, we might as well be comfortable."


**The Church Fundraiser Trap**

*POV: Maybelle Carter*
*Setting: Calvary Tabernacle Fellowship Hall, Dusty Springs*

There was no battlefield quite like a church fundraiser.
The gossip was disguised as prayer requests.
The sabotage came frosted in cream cheese.

And if you listened hard enough, the tambourines weren't shaking—they were whispering.

Maybelle Carter stood by the punch table in a sea of folding chairs and judgmental stares. The walls of **Calvary Tabernacle Fellowship Hall** were lined with hand-drawn signs that read things like:

**"Fund the Future—Buy a Slice for the Savior!"**
**"Cinnamon Belle Presents: Healing Through Bake Sale Blessings."**
**"All Proceeds Go to Community Enlightenment (and Some Overhead)."**

Translation: she was about to **launder bad press with banana pudding**.

Cinnamon Belle stood at the center of the room, wearing a white linen dress and a halo of faux humility. Her voice rose above the murmuring crowd:

"Thank you for coming, blessed souls. Today, we feed both body and spirit—and raise funds for our Community Crystal Literacy Project."

Maybelle sipped the church punch—glow-in-the-dark red and sweet enough to wake the diabetic dead. She scanned the room. The trap was already set.

Sister Velma was seated near the raffle table, pretending to crochet. Her brooch was blinking softly, camera active.

Ronny was at the DJ booth, playing gospel trap remixes and passing out QR-coded stickers that linked to **"Cinnamon Belle: Unfiltered and Unhinged – A TikTok Documentary."**

Even Quita was here, wearing a "#TeamNana" pin camouflaged in rhinestones, and standing by the pie table like an undercover agent of chaos.

Maybelle's job? Get Cinnamon talking. Bragging. Slipping.

She walked up to the "blessing table" where Cinnamon was organizing stacks of donation envelopes.

"Well, look at you," Maybelle said with a smile that could slice through Kevlar. "Turning holy carbs into campaign cash. Jesus would've made loaves, but you? You made lemonade stands for your ego."

Cinnamon blinked, then composed herself.

"Maybelle," she said sweetly. "Still following Nana around like a backup tambourine?"

"Oh, I follow no one. But I do *audit the math* when spiritual folks start counting donations before the Lord says amen."

Cinnamon laughed too loudly. "Oh, don't be bitter. We're just raising *awareness* today. For the children."

"Which children?" Maybelle tilted her head. "The actual ones? Or your side hustle recruits who think 'chakra alignment' is covered by Medicare?"

Cinnamon bristled.

"All donations go through a third-party trust," she said stiffly. "Handled by my campaign's spiritual treasurer."

"And who's that?" Maybelle asked.

"Pastor D-Stacks."

Velma's brooch blinked harder.

Ronny muttered from the booth: "Got her."

Maybelle leaned in, voice sugar-sweet. "You mean the same D-Stacks who got caught last year writing himself love letters from fake tithers in prison?"

Cinnamon froze.

Someone nearby gasped. A cookie dropped. A fan snapped open in reflexive spiritual defense.

"I... I wasn't aware of that," Cinnamon stammered.

"Awareness is key," Maybelle said, plucking a lemon bar from the table. "That's what this whole event's about, isn't it?"

Cinnamon straightened her spine, forcing a smile.

"We're promoting peace, healing, and civic engagement."

"And receipts?" Maybelle asked. "Because you'll need 'em. Especially after this livestream hits the timeline."

She nodded toward Velma, who gave a discreet wave like a grandma revealing she just hacked the NSA.

Cinnamon turned pale under her filter-proof foundation.

Maybelle took a bite of the lemon bar. Chewed slowly.

"Hmm. Dry. Just like your public support."

She turned on her heel and walked away, her heels clicking like a countdown.

Behind her, whispers spread like wildfire.

"She used D-Stacks?"
"I thought this was for the kids!"
"Girl, I gave ten dollars and my gluten flared up for THIS?"

Cinnamon stood frozen at her booth, watching her credibility evaporate faster than the punch supply.

74

Meanwhile, Nana May, who hadn't even shown up, was trending again.

**#NanaDon'tNeedNoBakeSale**
**#LemonBarsAndLies**
**#CinnamonCancelled**

## Pastor D-Stacks Falls from Grace

**POV: Nana May Jackson**
**Setting: Pastor D-Stacks' Private Office, Dusty Springs First Temple of Triumph**

His office was half sanctuary, half Vegas.
Velvet furniture, gold-framed mirrors, and a liquor cabinet disguised as a "blessed oil" closet.
Above his desk hung a photo of him laying hands on himself during a revival in '08. He called it "The Anointening."

Nana May didn't knock. She didn't need to. She walked in like judgment with a handbag.

"Derek," she said, her voice soft as a choir robe snapping shut.

Pastor D-Stacks—real name Derek Lamar Charleston III—looked up from his iPad, where he'd been halfway through a sermon and all the way through a cash app notification.

He smiled, but it was the kind of smile a man makes when he knows **his past** just pulled up in a sensible Buick.

"Well if it isn't Sister May," he said, adjusting his collar like it was suddenly choking him. "To what do I owe the divine interruption?"

"To your *pending rebirth*," she said, shutting the door.

He leaned back. "I'm a busy man."

"And I'm a busy woman. One with a file folder thicker than your third mortgage."

He blinked.

Nana placed the envelope on his desk. Labeled in tidy script: **"Insurance Policy – Mayoral Race 2025."**

Pastor D-Stacks opened it.

Out slid:

- A USB drive labeled *"Private Devotionals—You & Cinnamon"*

- Screenshots of text messages involving church funds, a hotel receipt, and two photos from his "miracle water" bottling plant in Alabama… which turned out to be a Dollar Tree storage unit.

"This is slander," he hissed, already sweating through his collar.

"Oh no, baby. This is *documentation.*"

He reached for his phone.

She reached for his hand.

"Let me stop you there, Derek. 'Cause you and I both know the only thing more dangerous than a preacher with a camera phone… is a Nana with *nothing to lose.*"

He sat down.

Hard.

"I'm not tryna get canceled, May."

"You already did. I'm just deciding whether it's *public* or *private.*"

Silence. Thick and holy.

She continued. "All I need is one thing. You drop your support of Cinnamon Belle. Immediately. And then you give a statement this Sunday: about redemption, about being deceived, about how the Lord revealed the truth to you through… let's say… a dream involving sweet potato pie and voter registration."

He looked up. "You're insane."

She smiled. "And you're almost famous again. Choose your viral moment."

He stared at the folder. At the USB drive. At the pile of sins that had taken years to compile and twenty minutes to arrange into political leverage.

"I have a congregation," he said, weaker now.

"And you can still have one," she replied. "They love a comeback story. But only if you jump ship *before* it sinks."

A beat.

Then, slowly, D-Stacks stood. Walked to his window. Looked out at the parking lot.

From there he could see The People's Pit BBQ. Someone had tagged a mural of Cinnamon Belle with a red stamp: **"False Prophet. Overcooked."**

He sighed.

"What do you want me to say?"

Nana handed him a pre-written press release. "Here's what the Lord revealed to you."

He read it. Blinked. "This is good."

"I wrote it during your third affair. You were always predictable."

He sat again. This time in surrender.

Nana turned, smoothed her blouse, and picked up her handbag.

"Oh—and Derek?" she said, just before opening the door.

"Yes?"

"If I find out you backpedaled, I'll release the tape of you crying during your own 'anointment massage.'"

He nodded like a man who'd just seen hell... and been asked to cater it.

She walked out with the soft tap of sensible shoes and strategic silence.

The church was quiet behind her.

But across town, her campaign office lit up with a phone call:

"D-Stacks just dropped Cinnamon. Said he was 'spiritually misled by modern mysticism.' You write that line?"

Nana smiled to herself.

"No, baby. That was just the *Holy Shade*."

## Cinnamon's Crisis Manager Quits

**POV: Cinnamon Belle**
**Setting: Cinnamon's Living Room / Makeshift "Spiritual Strategy Den"**

The curtains were closed.
The salt lamp was dimmed.
And Cinnamon Belle was in a kimono made entirely of recycled vision boards. She sat cross-legged on a meditation cushion that cost $189 and claimed to "rebalance spine chakras through hemp vibration."

Her phone buzzed again.

**37 new mentions**
**4 burner accounts tagged in Nana memes**
**1 video of her tripping over a protester's cat, now set to the Benny Hill theme**

Cinnamon took a deep breath. Clutched her emotional support geode. Whispered:

"Align… and transcend. Align… and transcend."

Then her laptop *dinged.*

Zoom login:
**Janice Waters – Campaign Image Consultant & Spiritual Brand Reclaimer**

Janice appeared on screen: hair tight, jaw tighter, holding a Starbucks cup with "THIS AIN'T MY CALLING" scribbled on it in Sharpie.

"Cinnamon," she said. "We need to talk."

"I was just finishing my micro-moon bath ritual," Cinnamon said with a smile.

"You're in your living room and that's a space heater."

Cinnamon frowned. "It's about energy, Janice."

"No. It's about *optics.* And right now, your campaign looks like a fever dream inside a Whole Foods dumpster fire."

Cinnamon sniffed. "The fundraiser was fine!"

"The fundraiser was a sting operation. We're trending under **#BlessedAndPressed**. Do you even know what's circulating on TikTok right now?"

"No."

Janice pulled up a video.

It was **Sister Velma's hidden camera footage**—Cinnamon accepting cash envelopes while saying, "It's not bribery if it's intention-based."

Cinnamon gasped. "That's out of context!"

Janice blinked. "You were wearing a crystal crown and said you were 'channeling Cleopatra's fiscal wisdom.' You're lucky you haven't been audited *by a pharaoh.*"

Silence.

"Okay," Cinnamon said finally. "So we pivot."

Janice took a slow sip of her coffee. "You want to hear the newest crisis?"

Cinnamon nodded.

Janice shared her screen.

It was a screenshot of a Reddit thread:

**"AITA for reporting my old spiritual coach who told me to insert quartz eggs for 'womb wisdom' and now I can't stop singing in Latin?"**

The post had Cinnamon's face blurred—but not enough.

"Oh God," she muttered.

"'Goddess,'" Janice corrected. "That was your whole brand, remember?"

"It was a *pilot program!* I told them to check with their gynecologist!"

"You also said the energy alignment would 'turn their menstruation into manifestation.'"

"I was being metaphorical!"

"You were being medically negligent."

Cinnamon threw her hands up. "So what? You're quitting?"

Janice sighed. Removed her earrings.

"Cinnamon… I managed a scandal where a senator got caught eating sushi off an intern at a campaign fundraiser. I fixed that. I even made the intern a brand ambassador for seaweed. But *you*…"

She leaned forward.

"You keep making *new mistakes.* You don't just trip on rakes—you plant them in your own damn driveway and bless them with moon water."

Cinnamon stood. "You can't just leave me!"

Janice closed her laptop halfway.

"You once said you don't *need politics,* because *'spiritual sovereignty is higher than democracy.'* So go manifest your way through a debate."

The call ended.

Cinnamon stared at the blank screen.

Then picked up her phone.

Started to dial…

Paused.

"No," she whispered. "I don't need them. I'll cleanse this energy. I'll realign. I'll—"

*Buzz.*
**New video posted: "Nana May Destroys Cinnamon Belle in**

**Sermon Freestyle."**

She clicked.

Nana was standing at the pulpit, saying:

"You can't smudge out stupidity. Some things ain't demons—they're just bad decisions with glitter."

The crowd went wild.

Cinnamon Belle sat back on her cushion, suddenly very still.

Even the salt lamp dimmed a little more—like it didn't want to be involved anymore.


## The Great Facebook Flame War

**POV: Ronny "Razor" Jackson**
**Setting: Ronny's Barbershop / Dusty Springs Facebook Groups**

Ronny Jackson had two great talents:

1. Fading a man so clean he could show up to his own funeral and outshine the casket,

2. Starting an online fight so surgical it looked like group therapy until someone cried.

And today? He was doing both.

He stood behind his client, freshening a lineup, while his phone sat propped up on a ring light, live-streaming into **Dusty Springs Neighborhood Group #4 (No Drama Allowed—Except This Kind).**

**LIVE NOW: "Nana vs. Cinnamon: The Smoke-Off Continues."**

Quita sat nearby, answering comments.

Sister Velma scrolled her burner account—**@VelmaGotReceipts**—dropping links like a digital vigilante librarian.

The latest Cinnamon scandal had been posted with the caption:

"Sis out here blessing parking meters while Nana fixed the church roof."

The comments were chaos:

- "Nana put her own money into those school lunches. Cinnamon only gives out air hugs and free sage you gotta burn yourself."

- "Cinnamon told my mama to manifest her gallbladder back. Nana took her to the ER."

- "Y'all ever notice how Cinnamon only shows up where cameras do? 👀"

Cinnamon's defenders came in hot:

- "Y'all just mad 'cause she glows and speaks truth."

- "Healing ain't linear, and neither is her campaign trail."

- "Nana out here threatening pastors. That ain't leadership, that's a sitcom."

To which Velma replied:

"Honey, if Nana wanted a sitcom, it'd be called **'Law & Order: Senior Unit.'** And it'd sweep the Emmys."

The likes exploded.

Ronny uploaded a meme:

**Top Text:**

"Nana May: Fixes potholes with her bare hands."

**Image:**

Nana in superhero pose, holding a shovel, church hat on sideways like a crown.

**Bottom Text:**

"Cinnamon: Tries to charge you $30 to cleanse your steering wheel."

It went viral in under an hour.

Meanwhile, someone photoshopped Cinnamon into an ad for a fake essential oil line:

**"Eau de Ego: Smells Like Denial, Costs You Friends."**


**But then it got real.**

An anonymous account leaked Cinnamon's **campaign donor list**, revealing multiple checks from:

- An MLM skincare company under federal investigation.

- "Wellness Bros United," a podcast cult infamous for claiming ibuprofen blocks your third eye.

- A vape store that doubled as a crypto tutoring center.

Ronny highlighted the juiciest names, captioned it:

**"Nothing says grassroots like a pyramid scheme."**

He hit post.

Facebook exploded like it found Jesus and petty in the same breath.

Cinnamon's camp tried to clap back with an emotional live video titled:

"Let's Raise Our Frequencies and Not Tear Down Black Women."

Except she accidentally went live while adjusting her bra and muttering, "Where the hell is the damn incense lighter?"

The clip? Immortalized.
Audio auto-tuned.
Posted with the caption:

**"Vibes… interrupted."**


**Later that night, Nana texted Ronny:**

*"Y'all got the town talking. Is it too much?"*

He replied:

*"Ma'am, you're trending on ChurchTok and The Shade Room. We are entering cultural canon."*

Her response?

*"Good. Just make sure they vote. And tell Velma to stop using animated gifs of me dancing. That is not me, and I cannot twerk."*


**The Revelation Sermon**

**POV: Nana May Jackson**
**Setting: Saint Paul's Baptist of Dusty Springs – Guest Sermon Sunday**

Nana May wasn't on the program.

She hadn't planned to speak.

Hadn't brought notes.

Didn't even wear her "campaign pearls"—just her Sunday shoes, a modest floral print, and the quiet fury of a woman who'd seen fools prosper too long.

She was just supposed to sit in the front pew and wave politely while someone's niece read Corinthians and the associate pastor performed a spoken-word sermon called "Healed Through Heel Turns."

But fate—or perhaps divine irritation—had other plans.

Because fifteen minutes in, Pastor Judson, bless his arthritic knees, leaned over and whispered:

"Nana… my throat locked up. I need you to step in."

And like any true matriarch of Dusty Springs, she didn't ask questions.

She stood. Straightened her back. Walked to the pulpit like the altar owed her rent.


"Good morning, Saints," she began.

The room echoed back:
**"Good morning, Sister Jackson."**

"I wasn't planning to speak today. But God has a funny way of rearranging schedules when the truth's been ignored too long."

Murmurs. Purses closed. Phones silenced.

"I don't need to tell y'all the town's in turmoil," she continued. "Y'all got Facebook. You've seen the flyers, the footage, the foolishness."

A chuckle rippled through the room.

"But I'm not here today to drag nobody."

She paused.

"Well, maybe just gently slide 'em toward accountability."

Laughter.

"I've heard folks say we need healing," she said. "And they're right. But healing without honesty is just hiding. Healing without action? That's just branding."

*Mm-hmms* and *Amens* swelled around her.

"We got folks in this town claiming to cleanse your soul for $49.99. But let me tell you something—ain't no sage strong enough to erase what you won't face."

People clapped.

"Mercy doesn't mean forgetting. Forgiveness ain't the same as foolishness."

She raised her voice now—still calm, but commanding.

"There's a difference between spirituality and performance. Between community work and clout chasing. Between fixing what's broken and dancing around it with incense and Instagram filters."

Someone shouted, "Tell it!"

"I'm not perfect," she said, placing a hand to her chest. "Lord knows I've made mistakes. I've raised my voice. I've raised some hell. I've raised rent money for single mamas with no heat in December. But I never raised a dime pretending to be holy while pocketing unholy checks."

That last line hit like communion wine laced with truth serum.

"And I sure as hell," she added, "never tried to turn a bake sale into a spiritual Ponzi scheme."

Laughter. Whistles. One elderly man literally stood up and clapped.

"I love this town," Nana said, softer now. "I've seen it grow. I've seen it fall. I've buried people and I've baptized their grandbabies. And I'm not asking for a crown or a title."

She looked around the room, eyes locking with each pew.

"I'm asking y'all to remember what leadership really looks like. It's not fancy. It's not filtered. It's not pretending to float while real folks drown."

The room stood as one.

She closed her eyes.

"And to anyone watching this livestream or reading this recap on Shade Room comments later—yes, baby, I said what I said."

Cheers erupted. Phones lifted. Cameras zoomed.

Nana stepped back from the mic.

"Y'all vote with your heart. Vote with your head. But please— don't vote with your chakras. They've clearly been misaligned lately."

She walked offstage to a standing ovation, leaving behind the quiet hum of transformation.

Because sometimes the most revolutionary sermon... is just telling the damn truth.


**[End of Chapter 4.]**

# Chapter 5: Receipts, Reversals, and Family Reckonings

## The Family Dinner Ambush

**POV: Nana May Jackson**
**Setting: Nana's Dining Room, Sunday Night**

Sunday dinner at Nana May Jackson's house was supposed to be sacred ground. The table was long, the food was endless, and the invitation was an open one. But tonight, the air was different. It was dense not just with the smells of pot roast and smothered cabbage, but with the unspoken tensions of a family at war.

Nana stood at the head of the table, carving the roast with a gaze that missed nothing. This was her inner circle, the chaotic but loyal heart of her campaign. At her right hand was Maybelle "Mayday" Carter, her lifelong best friend and the campaign's de facto strategist. Across from her, Sister Velma Green, another friend from the old days, clutched her purse like it contained state secrets—which, given her role as the campaign's top mole, it probably did.

Her grandson, Tyrone, sat slumped in his chair, the prodigal son who'd caused half the drama but was slowly, painfully, finding his way back. His shame was a ghost at the table. Then there was Cousin Ronny, Nana's grand-nephew, a whirlwind of social media savvy and questionable fashion choices, who was currently setting up his phone for a "family campaign recap" on Instagram Live. And finally, LaQuita "Quita" Brown, a younger cousin with a sharp tongue and an even sharper mind for logistics, carried in a tray of mac and cheese like she was transporting the crown jewels. They were a patchwork quilt of loyalty, dysfunction, and shared history, bound together by the formidable woman at the head of the table.

Nana cleared her throat, commanding silence without a word. She served plates with ritualistic precision—roast, greens, macaroni, yams, cornbread. Each spoonful was an act of both hospitality and subtle power.

"Eat first," she said, her voice a calm anchor in the churning waters of the evening. "Argue later. That's how we keep the peace around here."

But the peace didn't last through the first serving.

Ronny was first to break it. "So, Auntie—what's the plan for the next debate? We gonna bring up Cinnamon's miracle egg MLM or go straight for her donor list?"

Maybelle shot him a look. "Let's keep campaign strategy off the menu."

Quita sipped her tea. "It's already on TikTok, baby. Dusty Springs has opinions. Half the church thinks Nana is the second coming, the other half think she's the last temptation."

Laughter, thin and nervous.

Tyrone winced. "You know they got a meme of me with a dunce cap saying 'I believe in crystals'?"

"You should've stopped believing after the second yeast infection," Quita shot back.

Maybelle tried to redirect. "Family, we are here to eat, to love, and to support Nana's run. Not to drag each other."

But the table had other plans.

Velma, ever the truth-bearer, set her fork down. "You running a righteous campaign, Nana. But people asking: How you gonna fix Dusty Springs when you can't even fix what's going on in this family?"

The room stilled.

Nana wiped her hands, calmly, and looked around.

"What's wrong with this family?" she asked, voice smooth but loaded.

A beat.

Ronny coughed. "You mean besides Tyrone? Or—"

Tyrone cut him off, voice low. "Don't start with me tonight, Ronny."

Velma pressed on. "We're fractured. Half of us don't talk. Some folks are here for the first time in months and it's not because they missed your greens. We got old wounds nobody wants to touch, let alone heal."

Quita chimed in, softer than usual. "We all got receipts, Nana. You taught us to keep 'em. But what good is proof if we never use it to fix what's broken—just to hold it over somebody's head?"

The silence that followed was dense, prickly, unspoken things pulsing under the laughter and the hot sauce.

Nana set down her napkin.

"You want honesty?" she said. "Fine. Let's have it. This campaign's got me out here fighting the whole damn city, and now I gotta fight my own kitchen too?"

No one answered.

She continued, voice rising. "I ain't perfect. Lord knows I made mistakes. Raised this family on hard love and harder lessons.

Sometimes I was too quick with my tongue, too slow with my forgiveness. Sometimes I kept secrets when I should've let them see the sun."

She looked at Tyrone, then at Quita, then at Maybelle and Velma and Ronny, each in turn.

"If you got something to say, say it now. We're not leaving this table with any more rot than what's already in the fridge."

A long silence. Tyrone stared at his plate. Maybelle dabbed at her eyes. Even Ronny's bravado faltered.

Then Quita spoke up. "You taught us to survive, Nana. But survival ain't the same as healing. We gotta learn to let stuff go, not just drag it behind us like it's armor."

Nana nodded once. "That's real. I hear you."

Sister Velma added, "You want to be mayor? Start with your own. Fix this. Make us whole."

The words stung, but Nana stood tall. She took a slow breath, let the air fill the room.

"Alright, then," she said. "First order of my new campaign: no more secrets at this table. What needs to be said, gets said. What needs to be forgiven, gets forgiven. We don't win anything—votes, respect, or each other—by hiding from our mess."

She raised her glass.

"To family—messy, blessed, and always worth the fight."

The toast was awkward but sincere. They drank, some hesitantly, some gratefully.

For a moment, the room softened. Plates clattered. Laughter, real this time, bubbled up as the tension thinned.

But somewhere deep inside, Nana felt the knot tighten—there were still secrets, still stories untold, and before the campaign ended, every last one would find its way into the light.

Tonight, though, they ate.

And waited for the next storm.

## Tyrone's Confession

**POV: Tyrone Jackson**
**Setting: Nana's Front Porch, after Sunday Dinner**

The evening was thick with humidity and leftover drama.

Tyrone Jackson stepped outside, letting the storm door close behind him with a soft sigh. The porch lights glowed golden over the peeling paint and the trailing scent of fried onions and baked forgiveness. It was quieter here—the buzz of cicadas, the distant laughter from inside, the hush of a neighborhood that always pretended not to listen.

Nana sat on the porch swing, slow and steady, her hands folded in her lap. She didn't look up when he came out, but she scooted over—just enough space for a grown man and all his guilt.

He sat beside her, knees wide, elbows on thighs, staring at the porch boards.

"You gonna sit there all night, or you gonna say what's been eatin' you?" Nana asked, voice soft as the dusk.

Tyrone ran a hand over his face. "I don't know where to start."

"Start with the truth. It's usually the ugliest part, so best to get it out first."

He chuckled, a hollow sound. "You ever feel like you're about to disappoint everybody who ever believed in you?"

Nana didn't answer, just rocked.

Tyrone looked out at the street, where the glow of streetlamps cast old shadows.

"I messed up, Nana," he said finally. "Not the funny kind of mess up. The kind that'll get you on the news. The kind that'll ruin everything."

Nana nodded once, patient.

"I was… desperate, I guess," he continued. "Lost my job last fall, tried to keep it quiet. Didn't want y'all worrying. So I started picking up side gigs, some legal, some not so much. Delivery, hustles, you know. I figured I'd fix it before anybody noticed."

She waited.

"One of my 'clients' turned out to be someone in Cinnamon Belle's campaign." His voice got small. "They paid me to dig up dirt on you. Not just campaign stuff—family, old secrets, even fake stories they wanted me to spread if things got tight."

Nana's rocking slowed. The air between them went cold.

"I didn't give 'em anything," Tyrone said quickly, his voice breaking. "I swear to God, Nana, I couldn't. I took their money, but I never delivered. But now they're threatening to go public—say I'm your fixer, your bagman, your 'enforcer.' Say you paid me to hush people up and handle your dirty work. They've got texts, emails—messages I sent while I was desperate, trying to talk my way out of a corner."

He wiped his face, eyes shining.

"I'm sorry, Nana. I should've told you sooner. I should've never let it get this far. I thought… I thought I could handle it on my own."

The swing creaked. Nana was still for a long moment, just breathing.

"Why'd you do it, son?" she asked gently.

He shook his head. "I was scared. I didn't want to look weak. Not to you. Not to anybody."

She reached over, placed a warm hand on his back.

"We all get scared, Tyrone. We all mess up. What matters is what you do next. You brought it to me. That's more than most folk ever do."

Tyrone's shoulders shook, relief and regret warring inside.

"They'll try to use this," he said quietly. "To hurt you. To twist everything."

Nana squeezed his shoulder.

"Let 'em try. You did wrong, but you did right by coming clean. That's what matters in this family. That's what matters, period."

He nodded, a heavy breath rattling out.

They sat together in the dark, two shadows linked by blood and truth and forgiveness—the world beyond the porch suddenly feeling a little less impossible.

Nana rocked again, the swing moving in gentle rhythm.

"Go on inside," she said, voice kind but firm. "Eat some cobbler. Tomorrow we'll figure it out. Tonight we rest."

Tyrone stood, wiped his face, and slipped inside.

Nana watched him go, the weight of his secret settling onto her shoulders. She looked up at the night sky, the stars faint behind summer haze.

"Let 'em try," she whispered, to the moon, the trees, and anyone listening.

She rocked, slow and steady, preparing for whatever storm was coming next.


**Quita's Power Move**

**POV: LaQuita "Quita" Brown**
**Setting: DivaStyles Beauty Supply & Social Club – Ladies' Bathroom**

There are places in Dusty Springs where God refuses to go without backup.
The *ladies' bathroom at DivaStyles Beauty Supply & Social Club* is one of them.

It smelled like peppermint lotion, weave glue, and secrets. And tonight, it was about to become the Situation Room for one of the pettiest counterinsurgencies ever launched in a stall next to a wig mannequin.

Quita was touching up her lip gloss in the mirror—not because she needed it, but because plotting is more fun with a fresh coat of "Cranberry Savage #9."

She wasn't alone.

Inside Stall 3, a woman named Tameka "MessyBoots" Jenkins was whispering like a church usher on a gossip bender.
And Quita? She was recording every damn word.

"I'm just sayin'," Tameka hissed. "Cinnamon's team already got the receipts. They paid this dude to say Nana sold him fake campaign merch and kept the profits. Said it's gonna hit Twitter tomorrow at noon with a whole slideshow and sad music."

Quita rolled her eyes so hard the lashes waved goodbye.

"Girl," Quita said, "if I had a dollar for every time Cinnamon tried to drop a fake exposé, I could buy the town and turn City Hall into a pole dancing museum with a Chick-fil-A inside."

Tameka flushed and emerged from the stall like she hadn't just committed political arson while peeing.

"You didn't hear it from me," she said, suddenly nervous.

"Oh, I didn't hear it?" Quita raised one brow. "Then what's this?" She tapped her phone. Screen still recording. Audio crispy as a church fan in July.

Tameka froze.

"Relax," Quita said, slipping the phone into her purse. "I'm not gonna use this. I'm gonna weaponize it. Like a lady."

**Three minutes later**, Quita was perched on a red velvet couch in the front of DivaStyles, legs crossed, nails clacking like Morse code. She was already texting Sister Velma:

Target confirmed. Cinnamon launching fake scandal tomorrow. Operation Clapback loading.

Then she pulled out a USB drive from her purse. Labeled: **"Cinnamon's Spiritual Bankruptcy – Vol. 1: Receipts, Refunds, and Ratchet."**

She plugged it into the DivaStyles community laptop.
Inside:

97

- Screenshots of Cinnamon DM'ing an MLM girl named ChakraLisa begging for fake testimonials.

- A voice note where Cinnamon whispered, "Do you think you can make a fake altar for the photoshoot? Just add some candles and like… an old bible or something. I'll sage it later."

- One very blurry video of Cinnamon trying to bless a 5G cell tower with rose water and screaming when she got shocked.

Quita grinned. This wasn't war. This was **art.**

Then she texted Ronny:

"Drop the video at 11:55 a.m. sharp. Let her try to beat that story with five minutes left on the clock. We gon' Bible her before brunch."

Ronny's reply?

"Oh we cooking. I'm making memes right now. Nana as Joan of Arc with a Glock."


**Back in the mirror**, Quita adjusted her hoops and checked her posture like she was about to accept a Grammy for **Best Petty Political Maneuver in a Bathroom.**

Then she turned to Tameka, who was still hovering near the sink, wide-eyed.

"Next time you plan to snitch for a check," Quita said, smiling sweetly, "don't do it next to a real one. Now get outta here and go light some lavender, baby. You stressed."

Tameka scurried.

Quita winked at her own reflection.

"You tried it, Cinnamon. But this ain't spiritual warfare. This is hood chess."

She walked out the bathroom like Beyoncé leaving a divorce hearing—with receipts, grace, and just enough perfume to make your man remember her name.


**The Devil's Dropbox**

**POV: LaQuita "Quita" Brown**

**Setting: A dimly lit corner of a 24-hour diner, smelling of stale coffee and desperation.**

Quita slid into the booth, her glitter pen tucked behind her ear like a weapon. Across from her sat a woman who called herself "Genesis." She was a former "healing assistant" from Cinnamon's inner circle, now with the haunted, vengeful eyes of a disciple who'd been spiritually scammed one too many times.

"She promised me a role as a lead facilitator for her 'Tantric Re-Parenting' line," Genesis whispered, wringing her hands. "Instead, I was refilling her diffuser and fielding DMs from married men she 'healed'."

"I don't need the backstory, honey. I need the ammunition," Quita said, her voice low and steady. "You said you had something that would end this."

Genesis slid a plain brown envelope across the table. "This isn't just ammunition. This is a nuke."

Inside was a flash drive. No label. Just pure, unadulterated chaos. "She filmed everything. For 'content repurposing,' she said. This one... this one is with Pastor Darnell. The married one. With the four kids and the youth group."

Quita's eyes widened. "You're kidding me."

"She called it 'Root Chakra Rebalancing'," Genesis said with a bitter laugh. "I called it adultery with incense. He paid her, too. A 'love offering' of five thousand dollars, funneled through the church's building fund."

Quita felt a thrill of cold, hard victory. This was it. The kill shot. She had already planned to release the dirt she'd gathered on Cinnamon's fake testimonials tomorrow, a strategic drop to counter their narrative. But this? This changed the entire war.

"Why give this to me?" Quita asked, her mind already racing, recalculating.

"Because Nana Jackson, for all her sharp edges, is real," Genesis said, her voice cracking. "Cinnamon... she sells healing, but she leaves a trail of wreckage. I'm tired of cleaning it up."

Quita pocketed the drive. "Consider your karmic slate wiped clean."

Back in her car, Quita plugged the drive into her laptop. The video file was titled: SacredIntimacy_PD_Final.mp4. She clicked play. Her jaw dropped. The original dirt she had was a firecracker. This was a tactical nuclear weapon.

"Oh, she's not just canceled," Quita whispered to the empty car. "She's about to be spiritually deported."

She immediately called Ronny. "Change of plans. Forget the fake merch story I told you about. That's on hold. I've got the motherlode. The kind of stuff you lead with."

"How big we talkin'?" Ronny's voice crackled with excitement.

"We're talking 'shut down the church, the campaign, and her Etsy shop in one click' big," Quita said. "I'm holding the other dirt in my back pocket for now. This is the priority. Get your burner accounts ready. We're dropping this holy hand grenade tomorrow morning at 7:32 a.m. Let Dusty Springs wake up to the sound of Cinnamon's career imploding."

## Nana's Late-Night Monologue

### POV: Nana May Jackson
### Setting: Nana's Bedroom, Just Past Midnight

The town was asleep.
But Nana May Jackson wasn't.

She sat on the edge of her bed in a silk housecoat, the one with embroidered roses on the collar and a tiny rip near the right shoulder from that one night she tried to make cornbread and fend off Jehovah's Witnesses at the same time.

The lamp on the nightstand cast a soft circle of amber light. It made her hair gleam silver and her face look like a painting someone forgot to frame.

On the bed beside her was a **shoebox full of folded letters**, church bulletins, and Polaroids from thirty years of birthdays, funerals, and baby showers—most of which she'd planned, paid for, and cleaned up after.

She exhaled through her nose. Not tired. Just… *soul-weary.*

"Lord," she said aloud, hands in her lap, "I know I don't pray the right way. I don't do all that speaking in tongues and flopping around like I caught the Spirit in a pothole."

She smiled slightly.

"But I do talk to You. And tonight I'm asking for somethin' I ain't asked for in a long while: *clarity.*"

She glanced at the old photo on her nightstand—her late husband George in his sheriff's uniform, grinning like the devil knew something.

"I got a family that's cracked like cheap china. A town that thinks 'respect' is a filter you can buy. A campaign being dragged through glitter and gossip, and I'm supposed to smile through it like a Baptist mannequin."

She leaned forward, elbows on knees.

"You know what's wild? I didn't even want to run at first. I just wanted to fix the streetlight outside the rec center and get that pervert history teacher fired. But then I saw how far gone we were—how much *bullshit* folks were willing to believe, how much smooth-talking snake oil passed for leadership. And I said: *Not on my damn watch.*"

Her voice caught.

"And now... now I'm the one holding all these broken pieces. Trying to glue together a family, a town, and maybe myself."

She rubbed her knees.

"I love them. Even when they frustrate me. Even when they lie. Even when they disappoint me like Amazon packages that come half full and two days late."

She paused. Her tone dropped softer.

"But loving folks doesn't mean letting them hurt you, Lord. You taught me that, didn't you? Turning the other cheek don't mean *ignoring the pattern.* It just means you ain't gonna match their madness."

She sighed.

"I got dirt on half this town. Power folks. Dangerous folks. If I wanted to blackmail my way to mayor, I could do it tomorrow. And they'd *thank me* for the privilege."

She looked at her own reflection in the mirror across the room—older, wiser, tired, unbent.

"But I want to win right. I want to walk into that office and know I didn't have to sacrifice my dignity or my soul. Even if the other girl got a chakra army and a soft voice like a sedated daycare worker."

She chuckled.

"I swear, Lord, if she says 'vibrate higher' one more time, I'm gon' vibrate my foot straight into her incense burner."

A beat of silence.

Then Nana closed her eyes, folded her hands, and let the stillness settle.


**After a long while, she whispered:**

"Give me the strength to keep going. The wisdom to stay sharp. And the peace to know that even if I lose, I told the truth and walked tall."

She opened the drawer beside her bed, pulled out a tiny velvet box, and opened it.

Inside was a gold pin shaped like a rose—her mother's.

She fastened it to her collar. Not for fashion. For armor.

Then she turned off the lamp and lay down, the streetlight casting silver shadows on her wall.

Tomorrow, the war resumed.

But tonight, the general slept with her honor intact.

**[End of Chapter 5.]**

# Chapter 6: Bodies, Bailouts, and Blackmail Baptisms

**The Cinnamon Sex Tape Scandal**

**POV: Cinnamon Belle**
**Setting: Cinnamon's Condo – Candlelit, Chaotic, and About to Be Cancelled**

Cinnamon Belle believed three things with absolute conviction:

1. Her "frequency" was higher than everyone else's.

2. Palo Santo could solve trauma.

3. Her nudes were art.

Unfortunately for her, Dusty Springs didn't see it that way.

The tape dropped at 7:32 a.m. sharp. Not a second earlier. Not a second late. Just in time for folks to scroll while sipping their church coffee and pretending they didn't see that $600 tithe deduction.

The title of the video?
**"Root Chakra Rebalancing with Pastor Darnell – Leaked (NSFW but Spiritually Enlightened)"**

Cinnamon's face was fully visible.
So was… everything else.
Pastor Darnell, married father of four and youth group chaperone, was also enthusiastically present—shirtless, cross necklace swinging like a metronome to sin.

**Cinnamon had just finished her morning affirmation:**

"I am a divine vessel of light and radical softness."

She opened her phone.

And immediately screamed.

"NOOOOOOOO!!!"

The scream was half banshee, half burning-Victoria's-Secret-catalogue.

Her assistant, Bliss (yes, that's her government name), burst in with a smoothie and three different sage bundles.

"I DIDN'T POST THIS!" Cinnamon shouted, eyes wild, wig slightly crooked.

Bliss stared at the video.

"Oh my goddess," she whispered.

Cinnamon was pacing like a raccoon on meth.
"The angles! The lighting! That was *not* supposed to go public! It was a private healing session! For content repurposing later when I launched my tantric reparenting line!"

"Girl... you were upside down and chanting *'open thy portal'* while slapping holy water on his chest."

"It was *symbolic!*" Cinnamon shrieked. "He needed emotional detox!"


**Dusty Springs, however, was already chewing.**

The group chats were aflame.

- "Sis summoned the ancestors and the pastor's pants at the same time."

- "That ain't reiki, that's a certified rating on Pornhub."

- "I watched it three times and still don't know if I'm healed or traumatized."

Ronny posted a meme with Nana holding a Bible in one hand and a bottle of bleach in the other:

**"Cleanse your timeline. Nana 2024."**

Sister Velma simply wrote:

"Welp."

And the church's First Lady?
She changed her Facebook status to **"single"** and posted a photo captioned:

"When your man cheats but Jesus still paying the rent."


Cinnamon tried damage control.

She threw on a silk kimono, fired up a ring light, and hit Instagram Live like it owed her rent.

"Grand rising, souls," she purred, voice shaking. "I know many of you saw a… *miscontextualized* piece of sacred footage circulating online. Let me first say: **I am still vibrating.**"

The comments were brutal.

- "So is Pastor Darnell."

- "Not her trying to spiritualize backshots."

- "Girl, the only thing you opened was the camera app."

"I was guiding a client through **intimate energetic liberation,**" Cinnamon stammered. "We must learn to let go of shame, especially when it's filmed from a compassionate angle."

Her follower count plummeted by 10K in under 6 minutes.

Even the bots left.

**By noon, Dusty Springs was done.**

Her sponsors dropped out.
The local yoga studio removed her headshot.
A bakery canceled her vegan cupcake order with a note that read:

"We don't serve hot mess."

And Nana?

She didn't even gloat.
Just sipped her iced tea, looked at the sunrise, and said:

"Let the church say... *ouch.*"

**Back at her condo**, Cinnamon collapsed on her meditation pillow, mascara smeared, ego broken.

"This isn't fair," she whispered.

From the other room, Bliss answered flatly:

"You fumbled the whole campaign... with your *coochie.*"

## Sister Velma's Churchyard Baptism Trap

**POV: Sister Velma Claiborne**
**Setting: Mt. Zion Missionary Baptist – Parking Lot of Petty Miracles**

The trap was set with all the grace and subtlety of a Southern Baptist fish fry flyer laced with Bible verses and judgment.

Sister Velma had been up since 4 a.m., re-ironing her Usher Board blazer and selecting her war bonnet—a wide-brimmed floral hat so fierce it could block sin and sunlight at the same time. She parked her Buick LeSabre outside Mt. Zion Missionary Baptist like it was Normandy, and she was storming it for the Lord.

And lo—here came Cinnamon Belle.

Looking like spiritual regret in Gucci knockoffs and oversized shades, her energy was scattered and her aura was cracked like a Dollar Tree crystal under pressure. But she still showed up, because Velma had lured her with a simple text:

"Let's talk forgiveness. The Lord loves a comeback. Meet me at Mt. Zion. Bring a white outfit."

Cinnamon had read it between sobs, a sage stick in one hand and a lavender latte in the other. She thought:

"Redemption arc? Yessss."

She didn't know she was walking into a trap slicker than a greased deacon in tax season.

**Velma greeted her** in the parking lot with a hug so stiff it could've been legally classified as shade assault.

"Blessings, baby," she cooed. "I brought my prayer team. We want to lift you up."

Behind her, eight elderly women in white pant suits formed a half-circle around a kiddie pool filled with ice-cold holy water, courtesy of Velma's grand-nephew and a pressure washer.

A folding table nearby held:

- A laminated Bible

- A Bluetooth speaker playing Kirk Franklin
- A live iPad streaming to Facebook and TikTok
- A donation plate labeled: **"Forgiveness Costs Extra"**

## Cinnamon looked around, frowning.

"Wait... this isn't the sanctuary?"

Velma smiled.

"We're doin' it *old school* today. Public baptism. Full healing. Full exposure. Just like your video."

The other women giggled behind their fans.

"Wait a damn minute—this is a stunt," Cinnamon snapped.

"No baby," Velma said sweetly. "This is **repentance with receipts.**"

## Velma clapped twice.

The Bluetooth speaker cut the Kirk Franklin.

The livestream began.

*Viewers: 732 and rising.*

"Family," Velma began, looking straight into the iPad camera, "we are gathered here in the parking lot of peace to pray for our sister in spiritual crisis—Miss Cinnamon Belle."

Cinnamon tried to back away.

"Hold up. I didn't agree to a livestream!"

Velma didn't blink.

"You agreed to healing. This is what healing looks like. Painful. Public. Possibly viral."

The church ladies hummed in agreement.

## And then?

## The questions started.

Velma's voice, calm and cutting:

"Miss Belle, do you regret weaponizing your womb in front of the Lord's children?"

Cinnamon stammered. "I—it wasn't—my yoni is sacred—"

"Did you or did you not oil up Pastor Darnell in a 'chakra alignment' that looked suspiciously like a baby-making backbend?"

"I was cleansing his trauma!"

"You cleansed his mortgage payments too, huh?"

Gasps. Laughter. A thousand screen recordings.

## Cinnamon finally lost it.

"This is entrapment! It's slander! It's elder abuse in reverse!"

Velma stepped forward, Bible in one hand, donation plate in the other.

"Sister, you brought a yoga mat to a holy war. We're just tryin' to help you reclaim your narrative—with **hydration.**"

Then she motioned to the water.

"Now go on and step in this tub. We can rebirth your reputation if you humble yourself."

Cinnamon took one look at the freezing water, the fan-fluttering aunties, and the number of viewers climbing like gospel choir notes...

And she **bolted.**

Shoes flying, lashes lifting, dignity trailing behind her like a broken incense stick.

Velma turned back to the camera.

"Well, folks... she ran from the water, but she can't outrun the truth."

The crowd watching online erupted.

#Halleleak was trending by noon.

**As Velma shut off the stream, one of the elder ladies leaned over.**

"Did you go too hard on her?"

Velma tucked her Bible under her arm.

"Chile please. If that woman can do splits on a preacher, she can handle a little cold water and conviction."

They packed up the pool, the donations, and their fans—and left the scene holier than they found it.

**The Blackmail Drop**

**POV: Nana May Jackson**
**Setting: Maybelle's Garage, AKA "Campaign HQ" – Late Night Power Meeting**

The garage smelled like motor oil, menthol, and old secrets. Half storage unit, half command center, Maybelle's garage had seen a lot over the years—three failed barbecue fundraisers, two divorces, and that one time Quita learned her baby daddy was also her cousin's landlord.

But tonight?

Tonight, it was a war bunker. And Nana was the general.

She stood at the folding table in the center of the room, arms crossed, staring down at a beat-up laptop with more files than a crooked DA's office.

Quita was there, leaning against a washer-dryer stack in a velour tracksuit that said **"Unbothered in the Lord."** Tyrone sat in the corner, quiet but present, flipping through a folder labeled **"Councilman Petty – Strip Club Receipts."** Sister Velma sipped a Diet Pepsi like it was communion wine. And Ronny was pacing like a preacher with Tourette's.

"This is a lot," he muttered. "Like… *Watergate with wigs.*"

"You damn right it's a lot," Nana said, calm as a courtroom verdict. "Y'all thought I didn't keep receipts? Baby, I got a whole **Dropbox of devastation.**"

She clicked the spacebar.

Up popped folders.

**"Cinnamon_Belle_Botox_Loan_Scandal"**
**"Judge_Henderson's_CashApp_History"**
**"PastorDarnell_SideBabyDNA_PDF"**
**"MayorCaldwell_Twin_Massage_Parlor_Visit_GPSData"**

And of course:
"ChurchFundKickback_2019_THROUGH_2023"

Ronny nearly choked.

"Sis. This is like… a political hitlist with footnotes."

Nana didn't blink.

"Every person who tried to break this town, humiliate my family, or buy their way into power left a trail. I just followed it… and saved screenshots."

She gestured to the printer in the corner.

"Printed hard copies too. For the old school saints who don't believe in the cloud."

**Quita leaned in, impressed.**

"Okay… but what's the play? We go full scorched earth? Leak it all and watch them drop like flies at a church potluck with bad potato salad?"

Tyrone looked uneasy. "Won't that make us the villains?"

Nana turned, finally speaking with that dangerous calm.

"No. It makes us the **mirrors.** If they look ugly in it, that ain't my fault."

Velma nodded slowly. "So what's the plan, baby?"

Nana exhaled, then slid two folders to the center of the table. One labeled: **RELEASE.** The other: **DESTROY.**

Everyone stared.

"I want y'all to choose," Nana said. "We leak one. Just one. A warning shot. A reminder."

Quita smirked. "A sample platter of karma."

"Exactly," Nana said. "Then we let 'em sweat. Let 'em know what I *could* do. That's more powerful than any speech."

She looked at each of them.

"I didn't come to play holy. I came to play fair. But I'm not about to let this town burn because Cinnamon wants to sell healing crystals dipped in cologne and lies."


They voted.

Unanimous.

**Mayor Caldwell.**

The GPS pinged. The receipts. The screenshots. The confession from one of the spa girls. All of it—packaged in a nice, polite .zip file with a timestamp, a burner account, and a scheduled drop at 9 a.m.

As Nana clicked "schedule post," the room went quiet.

Not out of fear.

Out of respect.

Tyrone looked up.

"You really think this'll scare her straight?"

Nana smirked.

"No, baby. But it'll remind her I'm not the one."


**As they packed up for the night, Quita paused by the laptop.**

"This whole time… you were sittin' on this kind of dirt?"

Nana slipped her coat on and grabbed her purse.

"Darlin', when you're a Black woman in politics, you don't wait for storms. You **build the levee.**"

She stepped into the night, streetlight halo catching her silver curls.

And behind her, Dusty Springs slept. Blissfully unaware that the morning would break with thunder.

## Cinnamon Goes Rogue

**POV: Cinnamon Belle**
**Setting: Dusty Springs Community Park – Voter "Re-Energizing" Event**

Cinnamon Belle was spiraling.

But not just *emotionally.* She was spiraling energetically, spiritually, and possibly geographically, given how many substances she'd ingested before sunrise.

Her morning smoothie had six ingredients—none of which were FDA approved—and her "Team Comeback" shirt was three sizes too tight and bedazzled with rhinestones that spelled out: **"NAMASTE OR NAH?"**

It was 2 p.m. in the Dusty Springs Community Park.

The sun was too hot.
The grass was too crunchy.
And the only thing higher than Cinnamon's frequency was her blood pressure from anxiety and oat milk foam.

116

**"This is a *voter revival*,"** she announced into the mic. "A moment of realignment. Today, we're not just casting ballots—we're casting out *doubt*."

Twelve people clapped. One was a toddler. Two were clearly just there for the free sage bundles.

Behind her, a mismatched crew of volunteers wrangled goats—yes, real goats—into a makeshift yoga pen made from campaign signs, jumper cables, and hope.

Cinnamon had dubbed it:
**"Grounding with Gaia: Goats for Governance."**

**As her phone continued to vibrate with headlines like:**

- "Pastor's Wife Files Lawsuit After Sacred Sex Tape Scandal"

- "Town Council Candidate Claims She Was Hexed by 'Karmic Yoni Queen'"

- "Nana May Jackson Spotted in Pearls and Petty Silence Outside City Hall"

—Cinnamon just… doubled down.

"If they try to bury me, I will *root and bloom*," she shouted. "We are here to cleanse the electoral field!"

She lit a bundle of mugwort and waved it around like a Walmart lightsaber.

Two goats fainted.
One woman coughed and asked if she was being pepper-saged.

**Then came the performance art.**

Cinnamon climbed onto a folding table, microphone in one hand, rose quartz egg in the other.

"We reject outdated systems," she proclaimed. "Paper ballots are colonizer tools! Real voting happens in the *soul.*"

"Girl WHAT?!" someone in the crowd yelled.

"Unbind your chakras!" Cinnamon cried. "Tear up your voter registration! Set your intentions instead!"

Then she began tossing voter forms into a fire pit she'd *absolutely* not gotten a permit for.

The goats started screaming.

Velma, watching from a parked minivan across the street, sipped a Capri Sun and muttered, "Yep. This the moment. We done hit batshit enlightenment."

Meanwhile, Ronny live-tweeted it all.

2:18 PM: She just threw a ballot in the fire and called it a "freedom scroll."
2:19 PM: A goat just peed on her hemp sandals.
2:20 PM: I think she tried to twerk but her energy said no.

**Back onstage, Cinnamon was now full tilt:**

"Voting is *low-vibration!* You think Nana gonna save you? That woman uses coupons and believes in bank accounts!"

People started leaving. Fast.

Someone threw a handful of wet collard greens.

Another yelled, "You just mad 'cause Nana don't need goat therapy!"

Cinnamon screamed into the mic, "Y'ALL DON'T DESERVE MY MAGIC!"

Then she slipped off the folding table, landed in goat poop, and fractured her campaign credibility in three places.

The livestream had 50K views by sundown.

The hashtags were brutal:

- #CinnamonToastTragic

- #GoatGate

- #BurningBallotsAndBrainCells

- #NanaWouldNever

That night, while Cinnamon soaked in a tub full of rose petals and delusion, Bliss handed her a note.

It read:

"We're pulling your campaign funds. Please seek professional grounding. And possibly a therapist."

Cinnamon stared at it.

Then at the mirror.

Then at the remaining goats grazing on her chakra chart rug.

And for once, she didn't say a damn thing.

# Tyrone Redeems Himself

**POV: Tyrone Jackson**
**Setting: Dusty Springs VFW Hall – Voter Registration Drive**

Tyrone Jackson used to be known for three things:

1. Having four baby mamas and zero reliable transportation.

2. Once claiming NFTs would save Black Wall Street (they did not).

3. Missing every PTA meeting but somehow never missing brunch.

But after a month of watching his mama take political punches, spiritual shots, and digital bullets from a failed Instagram priestess with goat privilege… Tyrone finally realized:
**You either help the legacy, or you stay the punchline.**


**So there he was.**

Inside the VFW Hall, in a collared shirt and jeans that didn't sag, setting up fold-out tables like a man with a mission and mild lower back pain.

He'd roped in two of his cousins, one of his exes, and a surprisingly fit Uncle Reggie who'd once tried to unionize the church usher board.

The sign out front read:
**"Get Registered, Get Fed, Get Right – VOTE WITH NANA!"**

Inside, they had free barbecue sliders, water bottles with Nana's face on them, and a DJ spinning old-school soul to make even the staunchest non-voter sway their hips while registering for democracy.

Tyrone was sweating but smiling. For the first time in years, he wasn't running from consequences—he was helping folks run *toward* change.

A young dude with a neck tattoo walked up.

"You the one who used to sell fake Jordans behind the Jiffy Lube?"

Tyrone paused.

"Used to," he said. "Now I'm tryna get you signed up to vote before they close your polling place 'cause somebody thought goat yoga was more important than civic access."

The guy blinked. Then nodded.
"Bet."


**By noon, the place was packed.**

Old folks. Young folks. Skeptics. Church ladies. One guy who swore Nana once beat him in dominoes *and* took his girlfriend in the same hour.

Tyrone greeted them all.

"Y'all ready to stop pretending your cousin's mixtape is gonna fix the city and vote for someone who actually shows up?"

The crowd laughed.

Someone shouted, "Preach, Nepo Baby!"

He grinned.
"I'm tryna earn the name now."

Quita dropped by with flyers and mac n' cheese.

"Boy, I don't know what's in that new deodorant you wearin', but you smell like accountability."

Tyrone chuckled. "I figured it was time I quit bein' Dusty Springs' favorite disappointment."

Quita winked. "You makin' moves, boo. Just don't let the power go to your head like Cinnamon did. She got goats suing her now."

As people lined up, filled out forms, and dropped their ballots in the sample bin, Tyrone climbed up on a chair.

"Listen up, y'all," he said. "This ain't about just my mama. This is about all our mamas, our grandmamas, the ladies who gave us rides, gave us shade, gave us bail money."

The crowd nodded.

"This is about fixing potholes and making sure the library don't turn into another smoothie bar with free Wi-Fi but no damn books."

Applause.

He pointed to the wall behind him where a giant banner read: **"Nana May Jackson: Respect, Receipts, and Real Change."**

Tyrone's voice cracked.

"She ain't perfect. But she's what we *need.* So let's give her what she earned."

By 3 p.m., they'd registered 114 new voters.

By 4 p.m., Tyrone got a hug from his oldest daughter he hadn't seen in weeks.

By 6 p.m., he drove his mama home in a borrowed minivan—windows down, music playing, barbecue breath lingering.

And as they pulled into her driveway, Nana looked over and said:

"You gon' make me proud yet, baby."

Tyrone grinned.

"I already did, Ma."


## The Final Face-Off Announcement

**POV: Nana May Jackson**
**Setting: Steps of City Hall – Facebook Live, Local News, and Every Auntie's Group Chat**

Dusty Springs had never seen a press conference with this many folding chairs or fried chicken plates.

Nana May Jackson stood on the marble steps of City Hall—not shaking, not sweating, but standing like Moses about to part traffic and *bullshit.* She wore her campaign pearls, a red pantsuit that screamed "elected and equipped," and a calm look that could end arguments and marriages.

Behind her: her crew.
To her left: Sister Velma in her church whites.
To her right: Ronny, holding a livestream phone like it was holy writ.
In the crowd: reporters, haters, undecideds, and one suspicious goat in a leash harness.

**She tapped the mic once.**

The feedback squealed like Cinnamon's last chakra reading.

"Y'all know who I am," Nana began, no notes, no fuss. "So I'ma make this quick."

She glanced at the cameras. "We've been through a lot. Political scandals, leaks, lies, livestreams, livestock…"

Laughter from the crowd.

"…But what this election's really about is respect. For this town. For the truth. And for the people who built it while half these other folks were busy fakin' enlightenment and tax write-offs."

She paused.

"And I believe if you gon' ask folks to vote for you, you owe them the **courtesy of honesty** and the **decency of public accountability.** So I'm calling for a live, public debate."

The crowd murmured.

"Neutral ground. Equal time. No goat interference."


**Velma stepped up, mic in hand.**

"And I'll be moderating."

A collective "OOOHHHHHHHHH DAMN" swept through the crowd like holy gossip.

Cinnamon, watching from her Escalade parked across the street, nearly swallowed her green juice whole.

Velma continued, calm and dangerous:

"See, I don't need a teleprompter or tarot deck. I need receipts, direct answers, and grown folks' language. No vibrations. Just verification."

Nana nodded.

"We'll hold it at the community rec center. Live-streamed. Transparent. Truthful. And a little spicy."


**A reporter raised his hand.**

"Miss Jackson, are you sure this won't just turn into more drama?"

She smiled.

"Baby, I run a family with seven grandkids, two exes, and a sister who believes the moon landing was fake. I *invented* chaos control."

A reporter yelled, "What if Cinnamon refuses?"

Nana turned straight to the camera, her gaze unwavering. "Then we'll take her silence as her answer."

Another reporter from the local paper chimed in, "Ms. Jackson, your team initially said Sister Velma would be moderating. With all due respect, how can the public trust this to be an impartial debate?"

The question hung in the air, a direct challenge to the campaign's integrity. Velma, standing near the back, tensed up.

Nana smiled, a slow, knowing smile. "That's a fair question. And because I believe in transparency, I'll answer it directly. I trust Sister Velma with my life, but I will not give anyone a single reason to doubt the legitimacy of this election. The stakes are too high for even the appearance of bias."

She paused, letting the weight of her words settle.

"That is why we are making a change. To ensure this is a conversation rooted in undeniable fairness, we have invited an outside arbiter. We are inviting Judge Althea Hayes, retired from the Fulton County Superior Court, to moderate," Nana announced. "She is a woman of unimpeachable integrity, with no ties to this town or this election. She will set the rules. She will ask the questions. All we have to do is show up and tell the truth."

The announcement of Judge Hayes, a legendary and notoriously tough figure in Georgia law, sent a shockwave through the press corps. This wasn't just a pivot; it was a masterstroke. Nana had taken a potential weakness and turned it into a demonstration of her commitment to fairness. This wasn't going to be a mud-slinging match. It was going to be a cross-examination.

Nana finished, her voice ringing with authority, "I'm not interested in a performance. I'm interested in a reckoning. Let's see who's prepared for that."


**The livestream comments exploded.**

- "Nana just laid down the Uno reverse of politics."
- "Velma moderating? I'm buying popcorn now."
- "Somebody tag Cinnamon. She need to sage her courage."


Cinnamon, still sitting in her SUV, muttered through clenched teeth:

"This is a setup."

Bliss, scrolling the comments beside her, whispered, "Girl… it's a resurrection. And you might wanna RSVP with your dignity."

Back at City Hall, Nana finished:

"I'm not perfect. I'm not flashy. I don't do goat yoga or scream in the desert to find my inner power. I *know* my power."

She stepped away from the mic, but turned back for one final line.

"Now let's see if she knows hers."

**[End of Chapter 6.]**

# Chapter 7: The Debate, the Dirt, and the Damnation

**Velma's Gambit**

**POV: Sister Velma Green**

**Setting: A quiet corner of the rec center parking lot, moments before the debate.**

The evening air was thick with the smell of cut grass and impending chaos. Velma watched Cinnamon's Escalade pull into a reserved spot, the setting sun glinting off the chrome. This was it. Her last, desperate attempt to stop a train wreck. Taking a deep breath that did little to calm her pounding heart, she walked over, her expression a careful mask of a concerned elder.

"Cinnamon," she said, her voice low and steady, cutting through the pre-debate buzz. "Can we speak for a moment? Not as opponents. As two women of faith."

Cinnamon, adjusting her silk blouse in the reflection of the tinted window, was suspicious. But Velma's earnest, almost weary, tone disarmed her. "What is it, Velma? Come to offer a last-minute prayer for my downfall?"

"No, child. I've come to offer you an exit ramp," Velma said, her eyes pleading. "I need you to listen to me carefully. You need to step down. Tonight. Before you walk onto that stage."

Cinnamon let out a sharp, disbelieving laugh. "You want me to forfeit? You think I'm scared of Nana?"

"You should be," Velma said, her voice dropping to a conspiratorial whisper. "This isn't about her opinions on potholes. She has everything. The videos. The financial records.

The audio of you talking to Barbara Cain about leveraging the mayor's private life. Things that will not just end your campaign, but will follow you for the rest of your days. I've seen the files, child. It's a slaughter."

Velma was playing a dangerous, desperate game. She thought if she could just make Cinnamon see the sheer scale of the annihilation waiting for her, she would withdraw. It was a misguided act of mercy, an attempt to protect Nana from having to become the monster to slay the monster.

For a split second, Cinnamon's mask slipped. A flicker of genuine terror flashed in her eyes. She knew what videos Velma was talking about. But then, the fear was gone, replaced by a hard, glittering defiance.

"She won't use it," Cinnamon said, her voice a low hiss. "She wouldn't dare. The people would see it for what it is—a desperate, ugly attack."

"Don't bet your soul on that," Velma urged, placing a hand on Cinnamon's arm. "This isn't about what the people believe; it's about what they will see with their own eyes. I'm telling you this for your own good. And for Nana's. Walk away now, with your dignity intact. Don't make her do this."

Cinnamon yanked her arm away as if Velma's touch were poison. Her fear had hardened into a diamond of pure, uncut rage. "You think you can intimidate me?

You and your geriatric gang of has-beens?

You go back and tell Nana that her threats have been received. And you tell her that trying to blackmail me is the weakest thing she's ever done."

She turned and stormed off toward the rec center, a warrior marching confidently toward her own doom.

Velma watched her go, the cool evening air suddenly feeling frigid. Her heart sank. She hadn't prevented a war. She had just confirmed the enemy's coordinates and handed them a martyr complex.

The slaughter was still coming, and now, Velma knew she had failed to stop it.

## Pre-Debate Pep Talk

**POV: Nana May Jackson**
**Setting: Community Rec Center – Green Room (a.k.a. Mop Closet Rebranded as Political HQ)**

The green room smelled like expired Lysol, sweat, and prophecy.

It was technically a mop closet—rebranded for the night with two folding chairs, a ring light, and a mirror that had seen more breakdowns than a therapist with a group discount.

But Nana May Jackson didn't flinch. She sat upright in her red pantsuit, legs crossed at the ankles, hands folded like she was waiting to collect her crown.

Ronny paced behind her like a caffeinated meerkat.
Quita fanned herself with a campaign flyer.
Velma prayed silently in the corner, whispering the names of every petty spirit she intended to bind before showtime.

Tyrone leaned in the doorway, arms crossed. "You ready, Ma?"

Nana looked at him through the mirror. "Baby, I was born during a tornado warning in a sugarcane field. I been ready since the doctor smacked me and I slapped him back."

Silence.

Then laughter. Loud, needed, tension-cutting laughter.

"You know she dangerous when she start tellin' birth stories," Quita whispered, eyes wide.

Nana stood, adjusted her collar, and turned to face them all. "Alright, y'all, gather 'round and stop lookin' like you're waiting on a root canal. That girl out there thinks she's gonna cleanse my aura with sage and a soft voice. But this ain't a healing circle. This is a municipal exorcism.

And I'm not doing it for a title. I'm doing it for Ms. Henderson down the street who had to choose between her heart pills and her light bill last winter. I'm doing it for every kid who got a librarian instead of a laptop. I'm doing it because this town's been run by clowns in suits for so long, we forgot what leadership without a kickback even looks like. I'm here to remind them."

Velma opened one eye and said, "Then go on and cash that reality check, sis. It's been a long time comin'."

Quita pulled out a small plastic bag and handed it to Nana.

Inside was a delicate gold pin—Nana's late sister's campaign brooch from her school board run in the '90s.

"She'd want you to have this tonight."

Nana took it slowly, hand trembling just for a moment, then pinned it to her lapel.

"I already got her fire in me. This just makes it official."


Just then, a knock at the door.

A rec center volunteer stuck her head in. "We're live in five."

Nana nodded. "Tell 'em the truth's on her way."

As they all filed out, Tyrone lingered.

"You nervous?"

Nana looked him dead in the face.

"I'm not scared of Cinnamon. I'm scared of letting folks believe she's all they got."

She walked out before he could answer, leaving behind only the echo of her footsteps and the smell of Black woman magic.


## Cinnamon's Breakdown

**POV: Cinnamon Belle**
**Setting: Rec Center Backstage Holding Room – 15 Minutes to Show**

Cinnamon Belle was in full meltdown.

And not the cute influencer kind where you cry one perfectly symmetrical tear and then get a skincare sponsorship. No. This was full-on *spiritual hemorrhage in a sequin romper.*

The rec center "green room" assigned to her was less 'divine goddess retreat' and more 'school janitor's break room with ghosts of expired vending machine snacks.'

"WHY is this lighting so... WHITE?" she hissed, pacing like a chakra-panicked coyote. "My aura cannot be seen in this kind of violence!"

Bliss, ever the assistant-slash-handler-slash-crisis-sponge, stood nearby holding two ring lights, a makeup bag, and a Bluetooth speaker quietly whispering rain sounds.

Cinnamon spun toward her.

"Did you bring the aura mist?!"

"I brought four," Bliss replied. "Rose quartz, forgiveness blend, eucalyptus domination, and... the emergency one."

She held up a bottle labeled **'Don't F*ck This Up.'**

Cinnamon grabbed it, sprayed it around her head like it was oxygen, and took a deep breath that almost ended in a sob.

She turned to the mirror. Her reflection was... shaky. Too much concealer. Not enough confidence. Her highlighter looked more like anxiety sweat in HD.

"This is not how the face of Dusty Springs should GLOW," she snapped. "Nana is probably in her dressing room sipping peppermint tea and quoting Maya Angelou while wearing orthopedic boots made of moral superiority!"

Bliss hesitated.

"She's actually in a mop closet giving a speech about grandmothers and God."

Cinnamon blinked.

"What."

**Then the spiral hit full tilt.**

She grabbed a crystal from her bra—amethyst, supposedly—and pointed it like a weapon.

"I built a brand! I *aligned the town!* I made spiritual warfare SEXY! And now they wanna cancel me because a goat peed on my chakras and Nana's using senior citizen pity magic?!"

Her voice cracked.

"I burned ballots for *the culture,* Bliss."

"No one asked you to do that," Bliss said gently.

Cinnamon dropped into a chair like gravity had beef with her.

"I should've stayed in Atlanta and married that Scorpio podiatrist."

"You dumped him because he wouldn't build a moon circle sauna with you."

"HE LACKED VISION."

**There was a knock at the door.**

"Five minutes, Miss Belle."

Cinnamon leapt up and started pacing again, then froze.

"Do you think... she's gonna bring up the video?"

Bliss said nothing.

"…The church one or the Vegas one?" she added quietly.

Still silence.

"Oh, my goddess. I'm going to die on livestream."

"You're not going to die," Bliss sighed, brushing some glitter off her shoulder. "You're just going to answer questions. Like an adult. With boundaries. And zero mention of goat politics."

Cinnamon stood tall, adjusted her straps, and whispered to her own reflection:

"You are light. You are love. You are legally untouchable."

Then, with one last spray of aura mist and a shaky smile, she headed toward the stage.

Bliss followed behind her, whispering what she hoped were calming affirmations but were really just the words "please don't screw this up" on loop.

### Judge Hayes Takes the Stage

### POV: Omniscient

### Setting: Rec Center – Debate Stage (Live Broadcast)

The crowd was restless. The air in the rec center was thick with anticipation, smelling of popcorn and political bloodsport.

On stage, two acrylic podiums stood like sacrificial altars. But in the center, there was no rolling office chair for Velma. Instead, there was a formidable oak table, and behind it sat Judge Althea Hayes. She was a regal woman in her late sixties, with sharp eyes, a sharper mind, and a reputation for suffering no fools. She didn't look like a moderator; she looked like she was about to hand down a life sentence. Sister Velma sat in the front row, clipboard in hand, designated as the official "Community Fact-Checker," a role the Judge had approved with a curt nod.

Judge Hayes tapped the microphone. The sound echoed, silencing the room instantly.

"Good evening, Dusty Springs," she began, her voice deep and resonant, carrying the weight of a thousand verdicts. "I am Judge Althea Hayes. I am not your neighbor. I am not your friend. I am here as a neutral arbiter of fact. Tonight, we will have a debate, not a debacle."

She looked out over the crowd, her gaze sweeping across the room like a searchlight.

"Here are the rules. They are not suggestions." She held up a hand, ticking off points on her fingers. "One: Each candidate will have ninety seconds for a response. The clock is not a guideline; it is a guillotine. When the bell rings, your time is done. Two: There will be no personal insults, no name-calling, and no references to 'auric fields.' We are here to discuss policy, not peyote dreams. Three: If you make a factual claim, be prepared to cite your source. Sister Velma is here with a binder of public records. If you lie, she will fact-check you in real-time. You will be corrected. You will be embarrassed."

A nervous laugh rippled through the audience.

"This is not a performance," Judge Hayes concluded, her eyes locking onto the candidates as they walked onto the stage. "This is a job interview. And the people of Dusty Springs are the hiring committee. Let us begin."

She rang a small, brass bell. The sound was crisp, final, and terrifying. The debate had begun.

**The Debate Begins**

**The First Bell**

**POV: Mixed – Alternating Between Nana and Cinnamon**

Setting: Rec Center Stage – Debate Livestream Broadcast

The livestream chat flew by like gossip in a beauty shop: "#TeamNana"

"Cinnamon looks like she's about to manifest a lie"

"Judge Hayes is not playing! #GuillotineClock"

"I feel like Velma is about to object from the audience."

Judge Hayes adjusted her glasses, her gaze fixed and severe.

"First question. The city's infrastructure is crumbling, and the budget has been mismanaged for years. Specifically, what is your three-point plan to address the pothole crisis and the unaccounted-for funds in the Public Works department? Ms. Belle, you have ninety seconds."

The bell chimed.

---

Cinnamon Belle Cinnamon stepped forward, her smile bright and practiced. "Thank you, Judge. The issue isn't just about asphalt; it's about the very foundation of our town's energy. My plan is to first, initiate a city-wide 'Prosperity Prayer Circle' to cleanse the negative financial vibrations. Second, we will launch a 'Pothole Adoption' program, where citizens can sponsor a pothole and decorate it with positive affirmations. And third, we will divert funds from outdated, punitive systems and invest in—"

"Ms. Belle," Judge Hayes interrupted, her voice cutting through the spiritual jargon. "Your time is valuable. Do not waste it.

'Cleansing vibrations' is not a budget line item. What specific, actionable steps will you take to audit the Public Works department and secure funding for road repair?"

Cinnamon faltered. The pageant smile flickered. "Well, we would form a committee to explore holistic... resource allocation..."

DING. The bell rang, sharp and final. Cinnamon's time was up. She looked like she'd been slapped.

---

**Nana May Jackson Judge Hayes turned. "Ms. Jackson."**

Nana stepped to the mic, her presence solid as bedrock. "My plan is simple.

One: An immediate, independent forensic audit of the last five years of the Public Works budget, conducted by an outside firm. The results will be made public on day one.

Two: I will freeze all non-essential spending in that department until the audit is complete. No more 'consulting fees' for the mayor's cousin.

Three: I will reallocate the $1.4 million from the 'Civic Beautification' slush fund—the one that paid for the mayor's golf retreat—directly to road crews. We will start repairs in the most neglected neighborhoods first. Not the wealthiest."

She finished with ten seconds to spare. The crowd murmured in approval.

"Ms. Belle mentioned diverting funds," Judge Hayes noted. "Ms. Jackson, from where would you divert funds?"

"From the bloated salaries of do-nothing deputies and the phony non-profits that have been draining this city for a decade," Nana said without missing a beat. "I have a list."

In the front row, Velma held up a thick binder labeled "Public Records" and nodded slowly. The message was clear: the receipts were present and accounted for. The debate had found its rhythm, and it was the steady, punishing drumbeat of facts.

### The Reveal; Exhibit A

### POV: Mixed – Nana, Cinnamon, Judge Hayes Setting: Rec Center Stage – Mid-Debate Livestream Broadcast

The quiet in the rec center was heavy, judicial.

Judge Hayes turned to the next topic. "This question concerns leadership and character. Ms. Belle, you have positioned yourself as a healer for this community. Ms. Jackson, your opponents have characterized your methods as divisive. How do you respond to the assertion that true leadership must unify, not divide?"

Cinnamon seized the opportunity, her voice dripping with sanctimonious sincerity. "Thank you, Judge. True leadership is about healing. It's about raising the collective frequency, not tearing people down with negativity and anger. My campaign is about love, light, and bringing people together. It is a shame that some would rather resort to bullying and blackmail than engage in a conversation of ideas." She shot a pointed look at Nana.

The bell rang. Judge Hayes turned to Nana. "Ms. Jackson, your rebuttal."

Nana walked to the podium. She didn't look at Cinnamon. She looked at Judge Hayes. "Your Honor, I agree that leadership is about healing. But you cannot heal a wound by covering it with a bandage of pretty words. You have to clean it out first. And sometimes, that stings."

She paused, then continued. "Ms. Belle has presented herself as a healer. As a leader of unimpeachable character. I would like to submit evidence to the contrary, directly pertaining to her fitness for the office she seeks."

Judge Hayes leaned forward, her interest piqued. "This is not a courtroom, Ms. Jackson. But the voters are a jury. If you have relevant evidence, present it. Briefly."

Nana nodded once. From her jacket pocket, she pulled a small, unlabeled flash drive. She gave it to Ronny, who was standing by the tech table. "Exhibit A," she said, her voice even.

**The screen behind the candidates flickered to life.**

Clip 1: Cinnamon, in a hotel suite, whispering to a married city councilman, "If you don't vote against that housing bill, I'll tell your wife what we did with that chakra candle."

Clip 2: A text exchange from Cinnamon to her backer, Barbara Cain: "Don't worry, I'll keep the mayor's dick-pics encrypted. Unless I need leverage."

Clip 3: A recorded Zoom call where Cinnamon laughed and said, "I don't believe in taxes. I believe in tithes for the spiritually evolved. Plus, you can't trace Venmo rituals."

The crowd gasped. The livestream chat exploded. Cinnamon's face went from pale to crimson.

"This is an outrage!" she shrieked, lunging toward the tech table. "That is a violation of my privacy! It's slander! It's illegally obtained!"

BANG! Judge Hayes slammed her gavel on the table. The sound cracked through the chaos like a gunshot. "Order! Ms. Belle, you will return to your podium."

Cinnamon froze, trembling with rage and humiliation.

Judge Hayes's eyes were like chips of ice. "Ms. Belle, the legality of these recordings may be a matter for another venue. However, for the purposes of this debate—and for the voters of Dusty Springs—the question is one of authenticity. Do you deny that it is you in these recordings?"

Cinnamon opened her mouth, but no sound came out. She stared out at the sea of faces, at the cameras, at the undeniable proof of her own hypocrisy playing on a loop. The silence in the rec center was a physical weight.

"Ms. Belle?" Judge Hayes pressed, her voice leaving no room for evasion.

Finally, Cinnamon spoke, but her voice was a thin, ragged whisper. "This... this is not healing. This is a public execution."

"The truth is not an executioner, Ms. Belle," Judge Hayes said calmly. "It is merely a mirror."

That was the final crack in the facade. Cinnamon's carefully constructed persona of a serene, enlightened healer shattered. Her face crumpled, not in sadness, but in pure, unadulterated fury and humiliation.

She ripped the microphone from its stand. "You want a show?" she screamed, her voice raw. "You all love this, don't you? Watching a woman burn!"

Without another word, she threw the microphone down. It clattered loudly on the stage, the sound echoing in the stunned silence. Then, with her head held high in a final, defiant act of performance, Cinnamon Belle turned her back on the judge, on Nana, and on the entire town of Dusty Springs—and walked off the stage.

The debate was over. The war, however, had just reached its brutal climax.

## The Walkout

**POV: Mixed – Cinnamon + Public Reaction**
**Setting: Rec Center Stage, Parking Lot, and Livestream Channels**

Cinnamon Belle was halfway down the steps before she realized her left heel had snapped.

It didn't matter.

The walkout had already begun.

No music. No fanfare. Just the sharp clicks of acrylic nails and ego shattering under fluorescent gym lights.

She passed Bliss on the way out. Bliss didn't move. Didn't speak. Just held her clipboard like a broken promise.

"Don't," Cinnamon growled through gritted teeth. "Not now."

Inside, the silence on stage was the kind that has to be surgically removed.

Velma stood slowly. Folded her notes. Gave Nana a nod. Then looked out to the crowd and said, without irony:

"Well, I suppose the debate is over."

And the room *exploded.*

Cheers. Shouts. A few gasps that doubled as testimonies. Quita threw her church fan in the air like it was confetti.

Outside, the camera crews chased Cinnamon's exit like it was the O.J. Simpson chase but with better lighting and more glitter.

**Livestream comments detonated:**

"She GONE lmaooooo"
"This why Nana been quiet the whole time. Strategic. Tactical. Petty Jedi."
"Her aura just packed its bags."
"#WalkOfNoShameCauseSheAin'tGotNone"

Cinnamon climbed into the back of her Escalade.

Slammed the door.

Bliss slid into the front, started the car.

"Where to?" she asked, voice flat.

"Anywhere but here," Cinnamon snapped, smearing her lip gloss across her chin. "Anywhere that doesn't have old ladies with war flashbacks and USB drives."

The SUV peeled out of the parking lot just as someone spray-painted "#NanaNation" across a plywood campaign sign.

Back inside, Nana stepped up to the mic.

"I didn't come here to win a debate," she said, calm as stormwater.

"I came to make it real hard for y'all to pretend you don't know the difference between pretty lies and ugly truth."

She nodded once, then turned and walked off stage to a standing ovation that smelled like church perfume and fresh barbecue.

Judge Hayes didn't say another word.

She just leaned over the mic, smirked, and whispered:

"And that's on transparency."

## The Aftermath

**POV: Mixed – Nana, Tyrone, Crowd Reactions**
**Setting: Rec Center Exterior, Street Outside, Social Media Echo Chamber**

The air outside smelled like popcorn, barbecue smoke, and revolution.

The crowd spilled out of the rec center like they'd just witnessed the second coming—or the finale of a telenovela where the villain *actually* got dragged.

Tyrone stood on the sidewalk, watching the town buzz like it hadn't buzzed in years. A kid ran by wearing a bootleg "Nana 2025" shirt someone had screen printed in the church basement.

"Y'all see that debate?" a man yelled.
"My wig shifted from all that TRUTH," said a woman fanning herself with a bingo flyer.
A group of Gen Z voters were already making TikToks set to the soundbite of Nana saying, *"You sell healing. I live it."*


Nana stepped out, slow and regal, holding her purse in one hand and a Styrofoam cup in the other like the spiritual mother of a town reborn.

A woman approached her, teary-eyed.

"You ain't just won the debate," she whispered. "You made me believe again."

Nana took her hand gently.

"Baby, belief is free. Action is what costs."


Tyrone jogged up beside her.

"You okay?"

Nana sipped her drink and smirked.

"I'm good. Cinnamon's the one who looked like her chakra went through foreclosure."

They laughed.

"You think we really got a shot now?" he asked.

Nana looked out across the town—folks honking car horns, waving signs, clapping each other on the back like the whole damn city just survived something divine.

"We don't just got a shot, baby. We got *momentum.* That's more dangerous than any scandal."

Back at campaign HQ—aka her living room—Ronny was already scheduling interviews. Quita was prepping a victory playlist. Sister Velma had removed her pearls, kicked off her heels, and was holding court on Facebook Live like a digital Harriet Tubman of truth.

Meanwhile, the Escalade carrying Cinnamon was seen leaving town limits by exactly five people, three cameras, and one dairy goat.

Her Instagram? Quiet.
Her TikTok? Silent.
Her OnlyFans? Still active, but now mostly angry comments from ex-supporters like:

"Girl, you need therapy, not incense."
"How you gone align chakras from exile?"
"Nana bodied you respectfully."

At midnight, Nana sat on her porch, alone now, watching the moon rise slow and high above Dusty Springs.

She didn't need to speak.

She didn't need to smile.

She just needed to rest her feet.

146

Because tomorrow? The real work begins.

**[End of Chapter 7.]**

# Chapter 8: Afterglow Ain't Governance (But It Sure Feels Good)

## The Morning After the Storm

**POV: Nana May Jackson**
**Setting: Nana's Porch, Pre-Sunrise**

The sun hadn't bothered to rise yet. It was still stretching somewhere behind the pines, deciding if Dusty Springs deserved another day.

Nana was already on her porch.

In her housecoat, slippers, and a satin bonnet that looked like it'd survived every political war since Carter. A chipped mug sat in her hand—black coffee, no sugar, just bitterness and backbone.

The air was heavy with humidity and new headlines.

She rocked slowly. The swing creaked like it was gossiping.

Inside, her phone vibrated on the table. Another notification. Another article. Another invitation to speak at some conference about "elder Black women in modern governance."

She didn't touch it.

She was still letting her breath come back from last night.

From here, you could still see the torn campaign flyers in the neighbor's yard—half "Vote Cinnamon," half "Pray for Mercy." There was duct tape on one, scrawled in sharpie: *"NANA BEEN READY."*

She took a sip and exhaled.

"Lord," she whispered, "I ain't ask for this crown. I just wanted my streetlights fixed and these babies fed."


The door creaked open behind her.

Tyrone stepped out, rubbing his face, hair wild with sleep and what looked like existential crisis.

"You ever gonna rest?" he asked, sitting beside her with his own cup.

"I rest when I know the town's in hands that don't sell moon rocks as rent relief," she said, smirking just enough to make him snort.

They sat there, listening to the cicadas start their slow choir.


Tyrone broke the silence.

"You scared?"

She didn't answer at first.

Instead, she let the swing move… back and forth, creaking like it was weighing her spirit on each pass.

"Yes," she said finally. "Not of the job. But of bein' what they *need* me to be and forgettin' who I *am* to me."

He nodded. "Yeah. That tracks."


From the street, a car drove past and honked twice.

Someone leaned out the window and yelled, "MADAM MAYOR!"

Nana didn't smile.

She just looked down at her coffee like it had betrayed her.

"Don't call me that yet," she murmured. "We ain't even counted the ballots."

Tyrone chuckled.

"They already counted your impact."


She looked out at the town.

It didn't look different.

The cracks in the sidewalk were still there. The broken sign outside the barber shop still flickered "OPEN" and "REPENT" back and forth like God was indecisive.

But she felt it. The *pull.*

The same one her mama felt when she led sit-ins.
The same one her sister felt when she ran for school board.
The one that said: *You ain't finished yet.*

She stood slowly.

"I got a town to rebuild."

Tyrone looked up. "On a Sunday?"

She shrugged. "God don't rest when fools are in office. Why should I?"

They both laughed, quietly, like people who know grief and joy sleep in the same bed.

The sun finally peeked over the trees, lighting her face in gold.

Not spotlight gold.

**Crown gold.**


## The Belle Burnout

**POV: Cinnamon Belle**
**Setting: Cheap Motel Room, Edge of Dusty Springs**

The motel room smelled like sadness, Febreze, and betrayal.

Cinnamon Belle lay face-down on a polyester comforter so loud it could trigger seizures in three states. The AC unit sputtered like it was trying to decide if she was worth cooling.

Her wig sat on the nightstand. Her lashes lay like fallen soldiers on a napkin.

On the muted TV: a news anchor discussing her collapse.
On her phone: a thousand missed calls.
On her soul: a gaping crater shaped like a goat, a dominatrix, and the town that un-followed her in unison.


Bliss sat in the corner scrolling through Reddit.

"They're calling it 'The Nana-nuke,'" she said without looking up. "Hashtag's trending. Also, your Etsy shop's been review-bombed by grandmothers."

Cinnamon groaned into the pillow.

"You think if I burn some sage and claim I was hexed, they'll forgive me?"

"Unclear," Bliss replied. "But the Southern Baptists union is suing you for theological slander."

Silence.

Cinnamon rolled over slowly and stared at the ceiling like it owed her money.

She was still wearing last night's romper, now stained in regret and expired coconut oil. Her bronzer had migrated. Her aura had evaporated. Her dignity had filed a restraining order.

"I used to run Dusty Springs," she muttered.

Bliss raised an eyebrow. "You ran your mouth. Nana ran the people."

Oof.

"Unhelpful," Cinnamon croaked.

She stood up, wobbling slightly like her chakras were drunk.

She stared at her reflection in the motel mirror—cracked, dim-lit, and brutally honest.

Gone was the goddess.

Standing before her was a woman with contour lines like war paint and eyes rimmed in consequences.

"I need to do damage control."

"You need a shower," Bliss said. "Then maybe therapy. Then maybe a job."

"I have a job."

"Manifesting isn't employment, Cin."


Cinnamon picked up her phone, scrolling past DMs of hate mail, threats, and a very specific one from Sister Velma that just said, "The Lord's watching you. So am I."

She found the contact she swore she'd never use again.

Her ex.

The Scorpio podiatrist.


She tapped the name. Hit send.

One ring.

Two.

Three.

"Hello?" said a voice she hadn't heard in years—calm, measured, deeply unimpressed.

"Hi… It's me."

Silence.

"…Cinnamon."

"I know who it is."

Beat.

"…I messed up."

"Again?"

"Yeah."

Another long pause.

She sat back down on the edge of the bed, picking at her cuticle like it might bleed out her shame.

"...Can I come back for a while?"

Click.

Dial tone.


She dropped the phone. Exhaled.

Turned back to Bliss.

"Do we still have that Airbnb credit?"

"No. You spent it trying to open a 'Chakra Disco Lounge' in Sedona."

"Damn."

She slumped back against the bed.

"I got nothing left."

Bliss shrugged. "Well. You still got me."

"That's supposed to help?"

"No. But I also brought Pop-Tarts."

Cinnamon reached for the bag, tore it open, and bit down like it owed her absolution.


Outside the motel window, a billboard read:

**"Vote for Dusty Springs. Vote for Nana."**

Cinnamon threw the Pop-Tart at it.

It bounced harmlessly off the glass.

Her reflection didn't.


## The Town Meeting

**POV: Sister Velma Claiborne**
**Setting: Dusty Springs Rec Center, Community Town Hall**

Sister Velma stood at the podium like a woman who had *not* come to play.

It was three days after the debate, and the town was still high on drama fumes. Folks had lined up outside the rec center like it was Beyoncé tickets and barbecue night rolled into one. The sign-up sheet for public comment was already five pages deep.

The folding chairs groaned under the weight of righteous opinions.

Velma adjusted her mic. It squealed once. She dared it to do it again.

"All right, Dusty Springs," she said. "Let's begin."


From the back, someone shouted, "IS CINNAMON STILL ALLOWED IN TOWN LIMITS?"

Velma didn't blink. "We're not issuing exiles today, Gerald."

Laughter rippled through the room.

A man near the front stood up, hat in hand, face earnest.

"I just wanna say—last week, I didn't trust no politician. Not Nana. Not Cinnamon. Not even that possum that ran for comptroller in 2017."

Velma nodded slowly. "And yet here you are."

He cleared his throat. "But after that debate? After seein' what that woman did with just her words and a flash drive? I believe again. I believe in... consequences."

Scattered applause. A few "mmhmms."

**Then came Quita.**

She strutted up to the mic in a leopard print blouse and an energy that screamed "funeral soloist with a vendetta."

"I just wanna say: Cinnamon had me bamboozled. I done bought moon water, yoni pearls, AND them spiritual potato chips she swore would align my digestive chi."

The room erupted.

"But Nana? Nana reminded me who I was before Instagram lied to me."

She pointed dramatically at the crowd.

"You cannot heal a community if you don't know how to answer your own damn texts!"

Wild applause.

Next came the conspiracy guy.

"Yes, hi," he said into the mic, "I still believe the goat was a plant from Big Pharma."

Velma leaned forward slowly. "Security."

By the time hour two hit, the crowd had gone from fired-up to fellowship mode. Someone passed out snacks. Somebody else passed out voter registration forms.

And all the while, Velma stood firm—equal parts pastor, referee, and librarian of vengeance.

She didn't just moderate.

She curated justice.

**Finally, she raised a hand.**

"One last comment."

From the back, a small voice piped up.

It was a teenage girl—head shaved, rainbow pins on her jacket, eyes wide and hopeful.

"I just wanna say… I didn't know someone like Nana could lead. I didn't know we were allowed to have leaders who sound like us. Look like us. *Tell the truth like us.*"

The room fell silent.

Velma smiled.

"Well, now you know."

As folks stood to leave, someone plugged in a speaker and started blasting **"Ain't No Stoppin' Us Now."** Chairs folded. Voices rose. Nana, watching from the back, just shook her head with a smile and mouthed, *Lord have mercy.*

Dusty Springs wasn't just voting now.

They were *believing again.*

## The Media Frenzy

**POV: Ronny St. James**
**Setting: Nana's House / Makeshift Campaign HQ – Living Room of Legendary Chaos**

Ronny hadn't slept in thirty-six hours.

His eye twitched every time someone said the word "brand." The living room had transformed into a war zone of sticky notes, ring lights, cold Popeyes biscuits, and half-open laptops playing twelve different interview requests on loop.

"I NEED QUIET ON SET!" he screamed, elbow-deep in Nana's scarf drawer trying to find something "elegant but defiant."

"I'm not doing CNN unless it's Anderson Cooper," Nana called from the bathroom.

"You'll do Anderson, Joy Reid, and the damn *Weather Channel* if I say so!" Ronny shouted back. "We're in the middle of a content hurricane!"

Bliss (defected from Cinnamon's camp like a Republican after a pride parade) now sat in the corner sipping tea and organizing the chaos.

"She's already a meme," Bliss said, scrolling. "One of her yelling 'I am the damn receipts' just passed 200K likes."

Ronny nodded while dabbing highlighter on Nana's cheeks with surgical precision.

"I need analytics. Click-throughs. Ad dollars. Can we monetize that goat footage yet?"

"Working on it," Bliss said. "Also, Fox News is running a hit piece. Something about Nana being part of the 'Gray Panther Uprising.'"

"Good. That means we're winning."

**The phone rang again.**

Ronny answered mid-eyeroll.

"This is Ronny, strategist, crisis manager, and spiritual therapist to the baddest mayoral candidate Dusty Springs has ever birthed—what do you want?"

A beat.

His eyes widened.

"The Today Show?"

He covered the phone and hissed toward the hallway, "NANA! GET YOUR GOOD TEETH IN. WE GOT HODA."

Nana emerged, still in slippers, sipping iced tea like nothing in the world could knock her peace out of orbit.

"You better not have me lookin' like no damn TikTok grandma, Ronny."

He turned dramatically.

"You are not a TikTok grandma. You are a *legend in orthopedic heels.* Now suck in your diaphragm, find your moral authority, and *smize with truth.* We're going viral, baby."

Meanwhile, the living room TV played news clips on loop:

"The political firestorm out of Dusty Springs…"

"…a dominatrix-turned-mayoral candidate who destroyed her opponent in a livestreamed debate viewed by over 2 million people…"

"…and now, civil rights groups and fashion bloggers alike are praising Nana Jackson's unflinching authenticity and bedazzled cane…"

"Her slogan? 'I don't want the power. I just want the mess cleaned up.'"


Back on the couch, Nana leaned over to Ronny, voice low.

"This ain't gonna be easy, is it?"

He shook his head, touching up her lipstick like she was about to testify before Congress.

"No, Mama. But you got the mic now. So whatever we say next? It better matter."

Nana took a breath.

Then stood.

"Turn on that camera. It's time we told the *real* story."


**The Power Lunch**

**POV: Nana May Jackson**
**Setting: Gertie's Grill – Main Street Diner, Lunchtime**

The bell above the door at Gertie's gave its usual pathetic *ding* when Nana walked in.

She adjusted her scarf, straightened her spine, and took her rightful place—*not at the counter, not in the corner booth,* but dead-center, at the largest table in the room. The one usually reserved for dusty businessmen with city contracts and bad cologne.

Today? It was Nana's.

Already seated were:

- **Councilman Edgar Price** – soft hands, weak handshake, always smelled like money and nervous sweat.

- **Barbara Cain** – owner of the biggest construction company in town and a woman whose Botox couldn't hide her disdain.

- **Hank Dillard** – real estate agent, poker player, unofficial king of small-town shady deals.

They were eating without her.

Rude.


**"You late," Hank grumbled.**

Nana sat down slowly, removed her gloves like she was peeling back centuries of oppression.

"No, baby. Y'all just early for your reckoning."

The waitress—bless her—set down a sweet tea without asking.

"Usual, Miss Jackson?"

"Yes, sugar. Add a side of patience. This gon' be a long sit."


**Councilman Price cleared his throat.**

"Let's talk policy."

"No, Edgar," Nana said. "Let's talk **power.** Then we can work our way down to policy."

Barbara snorted.

"You got no seat yet. What power you got?"

Nana leaned forward, eyes steel.

"I've got receipts, Barbara. Not just Cinnamon's. Yours too. I've got emails, texts, zoning deals you signed off on while pretendin' to be at a spa."

Barbara's jaw clenched. "You wouldn't."

"I'm too old to bluff," Nana said. "And too tired to beg."


Hank tried to chuckle.

"Now, now. We're all friends here."

"No, we ain't," Nana snapped. "You called me a 'PR sideshow' last week on a call you thought was private. I've got the recording. Your ringtone's a Toby Keith song and your password is still '69Chevy.' Grow up."

Silence.

Even the waitress slowed her pour.


**Nana leaned back, sipped her tea, and smiled.**

"I didn't come here to ask permission. I came to let y'all know: I ain't blocking progress. I **am** the progress."

Barbara crossed her arms.

"So what do you want?"

Nana didn't blink.

"Equity clauses on every development. Rent control protections. Transparency audits on the school board's budget. And you'll all *publicly* support it or I start reading aloud from my very colorful Dropbox."

Hank raised an eyebrow. "That's extortion."

"No, sugar. That's what happens when you get outplayed by an old woman who reads *everything,* including the fine print on your tax filings."

Councilman Price finally caved.

"We'll back the reforms."

Nana stood.

"Good. Now I can enjoy my meatloaf in peace."

She turned to the waitress.

"And tell Gertie to put this on *their* tab. I just bought the table."

**The Campaign Reborn**

**POV: Mixed (Omniscient, Crowd-Centric)**
**Setting: Downtown Dusty Springs, Spontaneous Rally on Main Street**

It started with a speaker on a windowsill.

One of Velma's grandkids rigged it up with duct tape and Wi-Fi theft. Blasted out Nana's now-iconic debate mic drop:
**"I don't want the power. I just want the mess cleaned up."**

Then came the bassline.

Then the block party.


Within twenty minutes, Main Street looked like Juneteenth met the Emmys and decided to throw a block party with voter registration booths, gumbo, and righteous indignation.

Kids chalked "NANA NATION" across the sidewalks.
Church ladies passed out cornbread and voter pamphlets.
Barbers offered free fades to anyone who registered to vote on the spot.
A car drove by with Nana's face airbrushed on the side like she was a mixtape cover.


Ronny stood on a folding table, directing volunteers with the energy of a caffeinated Broadway choreographer.

"You! T-shirts left side! You! QR codes for donations—*not* the Nana thirst trap ones, the serious ones! And YOU—yes, you with the goat—MOVE IT TO THE STAGE, he's the opening act!"


Nana arrived slowly, walking down the middle of the street like royalty in compression socks.

No entourage. No security.

Just purpose.

She wore her best church hat and a look that said, *I told y'all this town wasn't dead.*

As she stepped up to the mic someone handed her, the crowd quieted like a movie scene waiting for the monologue.

She looked around.

Breathed in.

Then:

"I didn't ask for this. I didn't plan it. And I sure as hell didn't manifest it. But here we are."

Applause.

She raised a hand.

"I ain't a savior. I'm a *mirror.* You see somethin' in me? That's because it's in *you.* Now let's get this house in order."

**Cheers erupted.**

Signs waved. A baby was lifted into the air like it was Simba. Someone fainted—could've been from heatstroke, could've been emotional catharsis. The jury's still out.

Ronny whispered to Bliss, "We just turned a grandmother into a movement."

Bliss sipped her juice box. "We always were. She just gave us permission."

Meanwhile, back at the motel, Cinnamon watched the livestream from bed.

Mascara-streaked. Puffed eyes. Wrapped in a blanket called **regret.**

On screen, a hashtag blinked:

165

**#WeRideWithNana**

She muted it.

And reached for another Pop-Tart.

---

**The Prayer Before the Storm**

**POV: Mixed Ensemble – Nana, Velma, Tyrone, Quita**
**Setting: Church Basement, Late Night Before Election Day**

The church basement was silent except for the slow drip of an old faucet and the occasional creak of old wood remembering younger days.

Nana sat at the folding table, eyes on a half-empty coffee cup. Her pearls were off. Hair wrapped. The armor was on the floor next to her cane.

This wasn't Mayor Nana.

This was *Maylene Jackson,* former janitor, mother of two, dominatrix on Tuesdays, and the last line of defense between Dusty Springs and the devil it already knew.

Velma entered first, carrying a tin of mac and cheese like it was sacrament.

"I figured you forgot to eat."

Nana nodded. "Been too busy fightin' ghosts and budget lines."

Tyrone came next, hoodie half-zipped, holding his laptop and looking like he'd aged a decade since the first audit.

"Guess who just found a backdoor into the city's development fund?" he said.

166

Nana arched an eyebrow.

"Lemme guess. It leads to Kenny D's yacht?"

"Nope. Pastor Ricky's second nonprofit. The one registered to a strip mall in Alabama."

They all groaned.

Quita arrived last, dressed in full Sunday armor: black blazer, Bible in one hand, Glock in the other. (Metaphorically. Probably.)

She laid a folder on the table.

"That's your speech, Nana. I wrote you two versions."

"One if we win?" Nana asked.

Quita nodded. "And one if we don't."

Silence stretched between them.

Four warriors. No armor. Just scars and spreadsheets.

Velma lit a candle in the center of the table.

"Y'all mind if I pray?"

They nodded.

She bowed her head.

"Lord, we ain't askin' for power. Just for clarity. We're tired. Tired of pretendin' like civics is clean when it's dirty as the river after a storm. But we came this far, Lord. So give us the breath. The will. The nerve. And if we fall tomorrow—let it be fallin' forward."

"Amen," they whispered.

Tyrone looked up. "You really think we can win, Nana?"

She didn't answer right away.

Then:
"I don't know. But I know if we lose—these kids will rise anyway. This town's awake now. I just lit the match."

Velma grinned. "You didn't light it, baby. You *are* the match."

They laughed.

They cried.

They passed the mac and cheese like communion.

And when the night finally ended, the city outside their basement still didn't know it was standing on the edge of something holy and dangerous and brand new.

But it would.

By morning.

**[End of Chapter 8.]**

# Chapter 9: The Day the Dust Rose

**Election Day**

**POV: Bliss**
**Setting: Dusty Springs High School Gymnasium – 6:05 a.m.**

The gym lights flickered on like they weren't ready for history.

Bliss stood dead center on the hardwood floor, holding two iced coffees, three pens, and about four million volts of anxiety.

The folding tables were already set. Voting machines sat like squat little dragons waiting to be fed. Someone had written *"WE BELIEVE IN NANA"* on the dry-erase board and underlined it with a rainbow.

She adjusted her hoodie, cracked her knuckles, and exhaled hard.

"Alright, democracy. Let's f\*\*king do this."


By 6:40 a.m., the line was out the door.

Black grandmothers in church hats. Teenagers with first-time voter stickers and nervous smiles. Workers in hard hats and neon vests. Moms with strollers. Guys with tattoos and conspiracy theories asking, "Y'all got snacks though?"

They came for *Nana.*

And Bliss was running triage like a civic ER.


"Ma'am, that line is for registered voters, that one is for same-day registration, and *that guy* is just trying to sell mixtapes again."

She pointed. Tyrone waved sheepishly from a corner.

Bliss sighed. "You promised no SoundCloud today."

"It's themed! It's called 'Ballots & Bangers.'"


At 9:00 a.m., a girl named **Jayla** approached her nervously.

"Um... hi. I'm trans. They told me my ID don't match my voter file."

Bliss didn't hesitate.

"We're not doing that today. Come with me."

She grabbed the election judge, a white guy named Rick who looked like if a stapler were sentient.

"She's got documentation. Fix it."

Rick squirmed. "We're just trying to follow procedure—"

"No, you're trying to follow discomfort. Try following the **law** instead."

Jayla voted. Bliss gave her a hug and a sticker that said *"My Vote Is Real, Even If My Gender Makes You Uncomfortable."*


By noon, they were trending on TikTok.

#NanaVotes
#DustySpringsRises
#GlitterBallotsAndGrit

Bliss ducked into the janitor's closet for a five-minute recharge. She sipped her coffee like it owed her money.

Velma called.

"You good, baby?"

"No," Bliss said. "But we're winning. I can *feel* it."

Velma laughed. "Good. Don't get soft now. You were raised in a system, but you ain't married to it."


At 3:15 p.m., Cinnamon showed up to vote.

She wore a red power suit, matching stilettos, and the smile of a woman who still thought hashtags were a phase.

She walked up to Bliss and said, "No hard feelings."

Bliss handed her a form.

"This line's for people who still have integrity. Yours is over there—with the ghost voters and disgraced endorsements."

Cinnamon scoffed. "Cute."

Bliss smiled. "So's karma."


By sunset, the air outside turned electric.

Someone brought speakers. The line turned into a dance floor. A local baker handed out Nana-shaped cookies. Ronny passed out water and pamphlets like a caffeinated poll fairy.

Bliss climbed onto a chair and shouted, "YOU GOT TWO HOURS LEFT. IF YOU AIN'T VOTED, GET IN LINE OR GET EXCUSED."

A cheer erupted.

Tyrone handed her another coffee.

"You think she's gonna win?"

She looked at the line, the faces, the fire.

"She already did."

---

**Barbara's Broadcast**

**POV: Barbara Cain**
**Setting: WDSN Local News Studio – 5:59 p.m. Broadcast**

Barbara Cain adjusted her wig and smiled into the makeup mirror like a villain rehearsing a eulogy she didn't mean.

"Let's give 'em something to talk about," she whispered.

The anchor next to her looked uncomfortable.

"Just remember, Ms. Cain—we're only airing this because it's legally framed as editorial."

Barbara winked. "Baby, this ain't editorial. This is electoral euthanasia."

---

At precisely 6:00 p.m., the **WDSN Emergency Broadcast Crawl** interrupted Judge Mathis mid-sentence.

"Dusty Springs voters—tonight we bring you a breaking exposé from longtime community leader and former council chair Barbara Cain."

The screen went black.

Then faded in:

**NANA MAY JACKSON: WHO IS SHE REALLY?**

Barbara's voice, syrupy and slow:

"She calls herself a reformer. A fighter. But behind the scenes... Nana May Jackson has *secrets.* Secrets she's never told the people of this town."

Images began to play. Grainy. Dramatic. Cropped tight.

- Nana in leather boots, standing beside an unidentifiable man.
- A photo of a black whip on a bed.
- A document—barely visible—stamped "Client Confidential."
- A blurry screenshot of a cash app payment labeled: "Tuesday Session."

Barbara's voice grew cold.

"What kind of woman leads with lies? What kind of mayor moonlights in *masks and shame?*"


Cut to Barbara seated by a fireplace like it owed her rent money.

"I knew Nana back when she was just Maylene—the housekeeper, the side chick, the hustler in pearls. Now she wants to run this town like a dominatrix runs a dungeon?"

She looked dead into the camera.

"Well, Dusty Springs... bend over."


Backstage, the studio staff gawked.

The anchor whispered, "Jesus."

Barbara grinned. "He's not on the ballot."

Then the next clip rolled—**a mistake.**

The footage glitched... and the raw feed slipped in.

Barbara mid-sentence:
"I don't care if it's real. Just make it nasty. These yokels eat scandal for breakfast."

The producer gasped.

The cut was immediate, the signal scrambled, but it was *too late.*

Someone had clipped it. Screen-recorded it. Uploaded it.

By 6:17 p.m., TikTok had turned it into a duet.
By 6:45 p.m., Nana was trending again—but as a survivor, a badass, a legend.

**#NanaKnew**
**#WhipsAndWins**
**#YouCan'tBlackmailAFire**


In her living room, Nana watched the entire thing on Velma's old TV.

Tyrone stood beside her.

"You gonna respond?"

Nana smiled. "Nah."

"Why not?"

She leaned back.

"Because every woman who's ever been shamed knows the sound of a trap snapping shut on the hand that set it."

## The Leak

**POV: Tyrone Dupree**
**Setting: Dusty Springs Public Wi-Fi Pavilion (aka the Library Parking Lot) – 7:13 p.m.**

Tyrone's phone buzzed with rage.

Notifications stacked up faster than a Sunday buffet plate at Pastor Ricky's yacht fundraisers.

- "Yo, Barbara done lost her mind."
- "Did Nana really spank a judge?"
- "Nana trending in Japan. Deadass."

He didn't flinch.

He sat beneath the blue glow of the free Wi-Fi sign outside the library, hoodie up, laptop balanced on his knees like a war drum.

Next to him: a box labeled *"Judgment Day Dropbox."*
Inside:

- 67 pages of unredacted campaign finance fraud

- 4 burner phone records tied to Cinnamon's "consulting" firm

- 1 email thread from Pastor Ricky negotiating "pulpit silence" for $25,000

- And a *video.*

Tyrone clicked upload.


The screen blinked.

One by one, files launched into cyberspace like whistleblower rockets.

Target: **The People's Cloud Drive.**
Link: **open-source, no password, no gatekeeping.**
Caption: *"We tried transparency. Y'all ignored it. So here's the flashlight. Enjoy."*

He posted it to:

- Reddit

- TikTok

- Twitter

- The comment section of a Cinnamon campaign ad

- And his mama's group chat


In less than seven minutes:

- 4,372 shares

- 83,000 views

- 612 comments

- 17 cease-and-desist threats

- 1 very confused Wendy's social media manager asking, *"Why are we tagged in this??"*


The *video* opened with Cinnamon laughing at a fundraising gala:
"If these fools wanna think I care about potholes, let 'em. Just cash the check."

Then Pastor Ricky, sipping cognac on Zoom:
"We keep Nana out, we keep the *flow.* No more of these 'audit' demons."

Then Barbara Cain, slurring into a phone call:
"Baby, I could sell snake oil to a snake. That town's too scared to look me in the eye."

The voice on the other end? *Kenny D.*


Back at City Hall, Quita stared at her screen, jaw locked.

"Oh hell," she whispered. "He dropped the whole holy mixtape."

Nana's phone buzzed. Over and over. Until she finally looked at Tyrone's post.

Then at Velma.

Then at the sky.

"Guess we just took off the gloves."

Velma grinned. "No, baby. We just found the brass knuckles."


Meanwhile, Cinnamon, Pastor Ricky, and Barbara simultaneously called their lawyers.

And their therapists.

And then each other.

It did not go well.


By 7:43 p.m., the local radio station changed its programming mid-song.

A voice came on-air:
"This is *Dusty Truth FM,* and tonight, we're not playing music. We're reading files. Welcome to *The Leak.*"

Tyrone leaned back against the wall.

Laptop closed.

Mission complete.

"Good luck sweeping this under the rug when I set the whole damn house on fire."

## Nana's Address

**POV: Nana May Jackson**
**Setting: Front Steps of Dusty Springs City Hall – 8:12 p.m.**

The night had teeth.

And the air around City Hall sizzled with the voltage of something raw, something breaking loose, something that wouldn't go back into the box.

Nana stood alone at the top of the steps. No spotlight—just streetlamps, phone flashlights, and the full damn moon doing its best dramatic lighting.

Below her, the crowd swelled:

- Students with clipboards.

- Elders with folding chairs.

- Working moms with kids on hips.

- A few confused tourists just happy to see free popcorn.

- And Pastor Ricky, Barbara, and Cinnamon… *watching from the back like ghosts who realized the haunting ain't going as planned.*

Velma handed Nana the mic.
"You want your speech?"

Nana shook her head.
"Already gave it. In every file Tyrone leaked."

Velma smiled.
"Then go do what you do."

Nana stepped forward. The crowd fell quiet, but the tension? That stayed loud.

She looked at the people. Not above them. *With* them.

Then:
"I didn't come here to beg you for a title. I came to remind you who you are."

Pause.

"You are the damn title."

**Applause. Small. Then rolling like thunder.**

She continued.

"They said I was too old. Too black. Too female. Too freaky. Too loud. Too poor. Too *real*."

She pointed toward the courthouse.

"And yet I'm still here. While half them bastards hid behind paperwork and publicists."

Laughter. Cheers.

"They aired out my private life like it was some kind of scarlet letter. Baby, I *wear* red like it's armor. I didn't run for mayor because I'm clean—I ran because I'm *scrubbed down in truth,* and y'all know damn well truth don't come tidy."

The crowd roared.

"They said I ran a dungeon. I do. It's called **accountability.** And it's got room for everybody who thought they could steal from this city and walk away with their wigs intact."

The back row started quietly leaving.

Nana's voice grew soft.

"I'm not running to save you. I'm running because *you* saved me. Every young person who showed up. Every auntie who fed strangers. Every ex-con who mentored kids. Y'all did this."

A pause. Nana's voice trembled—not with fear, but reverence.

"I just carried the baton. You built the track."

**She closed:**

"If we win tonight, it won't be a victory—it'll be a *receipt.* A receipt for every lie we turned into law. For every insult we

180

made into innovation. For every time someone said Dusty Springs couldn't change."

"And if we lose—then we go home, rest our bones, and *build again.* Because they can rig a vote, but they can't rig a people who've *already risen.*"

Mic down.

No music.

Just tears, fists in the air, and hope that felt less like a dream and more like a demand.


**The Tally**

**POV: Mixed Ensemble – Nana, Tyrone, Velma, Bliss, Cinnamon (brief)**
**Setting: Election HQ – The Jackson House Living Room, Converted Into a War Room – 9:04 p.m.**

There's no clock in the world louder than the one in a campaign war room on election night.

It ticked like judgment.

Tick.
Would they accept a black woman who didn't apologize for being right?
Tick.
Would power pass the mic or hold it hostage?

Nana sat on the edge of the couch like she was waiting on a mammogram and a miracle.

Velma was knitting. Not because she needed a scarf. Because it kept her from punching the air.

Bliss was pacing, chewing an already-murdered pencil.

Tyrone refreshed the county results page every 4.3 seconds. "Why are they still at 67%? Who the hell counts ballots on a dial-up modem?"

**Then came the moment.**

Bliss gasped.

"69% in. Nana's up… by **two points.**"

The room held its breath like it was afraid hope would get scared and run.

Velma muttered, "Don't trust nothing until it's tattooed on a baby's forehead."

Tyrone said, "Or at least confirmed by three different news outlets that ain't owned by Pastor Ricky's cousin."

**Then the door opened.**

**Cinnamon.**
Hair sleek. Smile gone. Heels silent.

Everyone turned.

Velma stood up like she might lunge.

"I come in peace," Cinnamon said, hands raised.

"Funny," said Nana, "you came for war every other time."

182

Cinnamon stepped forward.
"I'm conceding."

*Silence.*
*Like the whole room forgot how to breathe.*


"I saw the leak. The receipts. Hell, even *I* was surprised how crooked I'd become," she said with a sad little laugh.

"I ran for power. You ran for people. And I was wrong. You win."

Nana blinked. "You... actually mean that?"

Cinnamon reached into her purse.

Pulled out a flash drive. Set it on the table.

"More files. Pastor Ricky's burner phone dump. Barbara's second condo in Panama. Take it. Finish the job."

Then:
"You're not just winning an election. You're ending an era."

And she left.


They all stared at the flash drive like it was a holy relic.

Bliss whispered, "I feel like I just saw Voldemort cry."

Tyrone cracked a smile. "This town's never gonna recover."

Velma picked up the drive. "Good."


**The results updated again.**

93% in.

Nana: **51.4%**
Cinnamon: 46.9%
Others: noise.

Tyrone froze. "That's it. The last precinct is Nana's old ward. That's a wrap."

They screamed.

Velma cried.

Tyrone danced.

Nana?
She just exhaled.

"Dusty Springs," she said softly, "y'all ready to get free?"


## Scene 55: The Reckoning in the Parlor

**POV: Nana May Jackson**

**Setting: Velma's Parlor – Evening, a few days after the election.**

The room was too quiet. Not the comfortable silence of old friends, but the heavy quiet after a storm, when you're still assessing the damage. The election was over. The victory party was done. Now came the reckonings. The plastic on Velma's couch crinkled as Nana sat, the sound unnaturally loud in the stillness. It was the sound of a friendship straining under the weight of a secret.

Velma's parlor hadn't changed since 1987. Doilies. Faded family photos on the wall, all watching like a silent jury. Nana sat in the floral chair closest to the window, not as a candidate, but as the Mayor-Elect. The title felt foreign, heavy.

Velma sat across from her, her hands twisting a handkerchief in her lap. She knew this was coming.

Finally, Nana broke the silence, her voice calm but carrying the sharp edge of a razor. "I know you warned her, Velma. You went to Cinnamon before the debate."

Velma didn't flinch, but her shoulders slumped just a fraction, a small surrender. "Yes."

The word, small as it was, was a confession. It hung between them, a monument to a trust that had been cracked.

"I trusted you," Nana said, her voice dropping low, each word a carefully placed stone. "With everything. With my family. With the future of this town. You were my sister in this fight. My right hand."

"I still am," Velma whispered, her voice barely audible.

"Then why?" Nana's voice rose, the calm finally breaking.

"Why would you show our hand to the enemy? Why would you give her a warning I wouldn't have given my worst enemy?"

Velma finally looked up, her eyes filled with a pained, desperate sincerity. "Because I was trying to protect you, Nana! Not the campaign. You.

I saw the path we were on, the ugliness you were about to unleash to win.

I didn't want you to have to become that person.

I didn't want your legacy to be defined by that moment of destruction, no matter how necessary it was."

Her voice cracked. "I thought... I thought if she knew what was coming, she'd fold. Quietly. No mess, no public crucifixion. It was a misguided act of mercy. I was trying to save your soul from the stain of it all."

Nana stared at her, incredulous. She leaned back, the floral pattern of the chair digging into her back, and rubbed her temples where a phantom headache had taken up residence. "Mercy? Velma, that wasn't mercy, that was malpractice! You gambled with everything we fought for. What if she had been smart? What if she had twisted it, gone to the press and claimed we were trying to blackmail her? It could have cost us the whole damn thing! We would have looked like the villains."

"I know," Velma said, her voice thick with regret. "I was wrong. I was trying to be your friend when I should have been your soldier. I saw the two women—the one I've known for forty years and the candidate who had to be ruthless—and I chose my friend. It was a mistake."

**They sat in the quiet again.** The victory, which had tasted so sweet on election night, felt different in this room. It felt... costly.

"We won," Nana said finally, the words heavy as tombstones. "But now we have to govern. And to do that, I have to know who is in my corner, no reservations. I have to know that the people I trust will follow the plan, even when it gets ugly. Even when it costs a piece of our soul to do what's right."

She stood and walked to the window, looking out at the darkening street.

"I need soldiers now, Velma. Not saviors." She turned back, her gaze hard. "Can I count on you to be a soldier?"

Velma met her gaze, tears finally spilling over and tracing paths through her foundation. "You can, Nana. Always. I learned my lesson. The mission comes first."

Nana nodded slowly. The fracture between them was still there, a hairline crack in a foundation that had seemed unbreakable. It might heal, but the scar would remain. "Good," Nana said, her voice softening just enough to let a little grace back into the room.

"Because the fight ain't over. We just moved to a different battlefield."

## Winner's Circle or Witch Hunt?

**POV: Nana May Jackson**
**Setting: City Hall Press Podium – Election Night, 11:34 p.m.**

The crowd outside City Hall surged like gospel at a revival tent.

Phones in the air. Signs reading *"Mayor May"* and *"Whip the System."* Someone lit a sparkler. Someone else was sobbing. The rest? Screaming her name like it was both prophecy and battle cry.

**"NA-NA! NA-NA!"**

Nana stood behind the podium, flanked by her newly unified council slate: Velma, Bliss, Quita, and even a shell-shocked but useful Tyrone wearing a thrifted suit like it was battle armor.

She adjusted the mic.

Then paused.

She could have opened with a thank-you.

She didn't.

187

"There are people tonight who will say I won because I'm loud. Because I'm angry. Because I made enemies."

She leaned forward.

"They are correct."

**Applause.**

She raised a hand. Silence.

"I didn't run to be loved. I ran to make this town uncomfortable enough to *grow*. And now that I've got this title, I ain't interested in keeping it warm. I'm here to turn this chair into a seatbelt— because we're about to *accelerate*."

She held up the flash drive Cinnamon had given her.

"This here? This is the rest of the truth y'all weren't supposed to see. City contracts to cousins. Donations with conditions. Praise-peddling preachers. Developers treating neighborhoods like game boards."

Camera flashes exploded.

"I'll be forwarding this to the state attorney general, two investigative journalists, and *my nephew Ray-Ray,* who runs the town's messiest group chat. We're covering *all* our bases."

**A reporter yelled:**
"Mayor Jackson—are you promising a witch hunt?"

Nana stared them down.

"I ain't huntin' witches. I'm huntin' **parasites**—and baby, I brought salt, fire, and a legal team with insomnia."

**Laughter.**

Applause.

Then:

"You wanted a mayor. You got a mop. I'm here to clean."

**Another reporter:**
"How do you respond to those who say your past makes you unfit for public office?"

Nana didn't blink.

"My past paid the rent. My integrity paid the price. And every woman in this crowd who's ever been told to shut up, sit down, or sanitize her story—*this win is yours too.*"

**Someone in the back held up a sign that read:**

"The Dungeon Elected the Queen."

Nana smiled.
"Damn right it did."

**She stepped away from the podium.**

Velma leaned in. "So... what now?"

Nana looked out at Dusty Springs.

The lights. The people. The chaos still trembling from its old skin.

She grinned.

"Now?"

She slung her cane over one shoulder like a sword.

"Now we *govern like we give a damn.*"

**[End of Chapter 9.]**

# Chapter 10: Hope Is a Hammer (Now Start Swinging)

**The Audit**

**POV: Nana May Jackson**

**Setting: Nana's Kitchen – Two days after the election**

The victory party was over. The lawn was clear of folding chairs, the last of the celebratory brisket was gone, and the house was quiet for the first time in weeks. But the work had already begun. Nana sat at her kitchen table, which was now buried under stacks of city documents, a highlighter in one hand and a mug of black coffee in the other. Velma was across from her, poring over a preliminary budget report with a look of profound disgust.

The knock on the door was soft, hesitant.

It was Bliss. She stood on the threshold, looking younger and more vulnerable without the armor of campaign chaos. She held a single, sleek laptop against her chest.

Velma looked up, her eyes narrowing. "The after-party's over, baby. And we don't do second-line parades for folks who marched with the other band."

"I'm not here for a parade," Bliss said, stepping inside. Her voice was quiet but firm. "I'm here because you won. And now the real fight starts. I want in."

Nana stopped highlighting but didn't look up. "The fight you're talkin' about ain't got no livestreams. It ain't got no trending hashtags. It's got zoning permits, ethics complaints, and angry constituents. It's boring. And it's brutal. Why would you want any part of that?"

"Because of what you did," Bliss said, placing her laptop on the only clear corner of the table. She opened it, revealing a meticulously organized file system. "You didn't just win an election. You gave people a blueprint. I spent the last 48 hours compiling every promise you made, every policy you proposed, and every dollar you said you'd find. I cross-referenced it with the existing city charter and flagged every loophole the old guard will try to use against you."

She spun the laptop around. There were color-coded charts, spreadsheets, and a folder ominously labeled "Structural Rot."

Tyrone, who had been listening from the doorway, let out a low whistle. "Damn. She came with a whole audit."

Velma was still skeptical. "You did all this for free?"

"I did it because for the first time, I saw what it looks like when you're fighting for something instead of just fighting against someone," Bliss said, her eyes finding Nana's. "I helped Cinnamon build a brand. I want to help you rebuild a city."

Nana finally looked at her, a long, appraising stare. She saw the exhaustion in Bliss's eyes, but underneath it, she saw the same fire she recognized in Velma, in Tyrone, in herself. It was the fire of the fed-up.

"Governing is about follow-through," Nana said, her voice a quiet challenge. "It's about showing up when the cameras are gone. Can you do that?"

"I'm already here," Bliss replied.

Nana nodded slowly. A decision made. She pushed a stack of files toward Bliss. "Good. Start with these. These are the vendors for the Public Works department. I want to know who owns them, who their cousins are, and if any of them have ever had brunch with Barbara Cain. You have until noon."

Bliss's face broke into a smile—not of triumph, but of purpose. "Yes, Mayor."

As she took the files and found a seat, Velma leaned over to Nana and whispered, "That girl moves like a villain."

Nana took a sip of her coffee and grinned. "Thank God. We're gonna need one."

## The Transition Team

**POV: Nana May Jackson**
**Setting: Dusty Springs Community Center Office, Monday Morning**

The transition office was technically a repurposed storage closet.

Two folding tables. A busted fan. Three extension cords that looked like they were auditioning for an electrical fire. There was a moldy motivational poster on the wall that read:
**"TEAMWORK MAKES THE DREAM WORK."**

Nana stared at it like it had personally disrespected her.

"This room smell like tax fraud and mildew," she muttered.

Velma, clipboard in hand, didn't look up. "That's because it *is* tax fraud and mildew. You ready to build a government or not?"

The first to arrive was **Ronny**, hair perfectly slicked back, tablet in hand, carrying three iced coffees like holy relics.

"I brought caffeine and a crisis binder," he said. "We're gonna need both."

Then came **Tyrone**, late but with a box of donuts and an aura of reluctant responsibility.

"I was up reviewing city contracts," he said.

"You mean watching Judge Mathis?" Velma asked.

"Dual tabs."

The final team member entered with the confidence of someone who didn't wait for permission.

**Bliss.**

Former Cinnamon campaign staff. Now fully reformed, aggressively efficient, and deeply unbothered by anyone's opinion about it.

"I organized your Dropbox," she said, tossing a thumb drive onto the table. "Also, I started a TikTok campaign: #NanaOnDeck. We hit 50K in under three hours."

Nana blinked.

"You move like a villain."

Bliss grinned. "Thank you."

**Nana sat down at the head of the table—or what passed for it.**

"Here's how this is gonna go. First, we fire anybody who thought I wouldn't check their receipts. Second, we clean house like it's a spring revival. Third—we start building this government from *actual community.* Not cronies. Not cousins. Not people who owe me favors."

She paused.

"Except Cousin Loretta. She do make good biscuits and know how to file."


Ronny flipped open the crisis binder.

"Top priorities: ethics reform, housing oversight, education audits, and reining in Pastor Ricky's influence."

Nana's eyes narrowed. "That man got more money than morals. I'll handle him personally."

Velma added, "We need a budget task force. And someone to review the city payroll. Last I checked, the assistant zoning manager's making six figures and no one knows what he looks like."

Tyrone raised a hand. "That's Marcus. He DJ'ed my cousin's wedding. Weird dude. Loves sea monkeys."

Nana tapped the table.

"Fire him."


They worked for hours.

By the end of the day, they had:

- Drafted the **Ethics and Transparency Ordinance**.
- Scheduled three town halls.
- Sent warning notices to every department head with shady books.
- Installed a camera outside the office labeled **"Smile! Nana's Watching."**

As they wrapped up, Ronny handed her a new phone.

"This has an encrypted signal, GPS lock, and facial recognition. You're official now."

Nana stared at it.

"What happened to my flip phone?"

"It's in the Smithsonian under 'Elderly Bravery.' Now hush and log in."

She powered it on. It lit up with the campaign's new slogan: **"Truth. Grit. Nana."**

She smiled.

"Let's swing this hammer."


## The Secret Committee

**POV: Omniscient – Old Guard Viewpoint
Setting: Country Club – Private Cellar Room, Evening**

The basement of the Dusty Springs Country Club was colder than the hearts of most men in the room.

Twelve of them, seated around an antique oak table that once belonged to a Confederate general—and still reeked of bad intentions. The walls were lined with bourbon, tax loopholes, and ghosts of embezzlements past.

At the head sat **Eustace Hollinger III**, banker, patriarch, and living proof that generational wealth rarely comes with generational wisdom.

He cleared his throat.

"Gentlemen. And Barbara."

Barbara Cain rolled her eyes. "Spare me the chivalry, Eustace. I'm the one who bankrolls three of your grandkids' trust funds."


The committee was unofficial but well-practiced.

Every ordinance ever delayed?

This table.

Every zoning change that mysteriously benefited out-of-towners?

This table.

Every failed attempt to integrate the school board?

You guessed it—these wrinkled Goliaths in Dockers and denial.


"So," said Pastor Ricky, brushing lint off his pinstripe suit, "how do we remove this... woman?"

"She's popular," muttered Hank Dillard. "And terrifying. She roasted Cinnamon like she was a Thanksgiving side dish."

Barbara lit a cigarette no one was technically allowed to smoke.

"She's not just popular. She's *efficient.* She's already purged the Housing Committee and requested a full audit of church exemptions."

Pastor Ricky blanched. "The Lord's money is private business."

"She ain't scared of the Lord *or* your lawyers," Barbara replied. "And she's got half the town TikTokin' voter education like it's a damn dance challenge."

Eustace pounded the table.

"Then we remind them who runs Dusty Springs."

"And how do we do that?" asked Hank. "Buy her out?"

"She won't take a bribe," said Barbara. "We tried. She iced us with one look and asked if we preferred our hypocrisy grilled or fried."

They all shuddered slightly.

The room fell silent.

Then Eustace smiled.

"We don't beat her at politics. We beat her at **perception.**"

He pulled out a folder.

Inside: photos. Old ones. Nana's days as a dominatrix. Grainy footage. Shadows. Whispers.

"The voters love a folk hero. But let's see how they like a **scandal.**"

Barbara smirked. "So we're going full smear campaign?"

Ricky grinned. "Praise the Lord and pass the oppo research."

A toast was raised.

"To tradition."

But the bourbon tasted like desperation.

And they all knew it.

**The Audit**

**POV: Tyrone Dupree**
**Setting: Dusty Springs Unified School District, Records Department – Late Afternoon**

The fluorescent lights buzzed like they were gossiping.

Tyrone stood in a beige room that smelled like expired toner and broken promises. File cabinets lined the walls like silent snitches. A printer blinked out of paper. Somewhere, a mouse squeaked. Possibly metaphorical. Possibly literal.

He adjusted his cheap tie and muttered to himself, "We are professionals now. Professionals who audit. Ain't no mixtape. Just spreadsheets. Spreadsheets of doom."


Across the table sat **Ms. LaThonda**, school board admin, queen of side-eyes, and gatekeeper of the tea.

"You ain't media, are you?" she asked, arms crossed.

"No, ma'am. Official mayoral review task force."

"Hmph. Y'all always say that 'til the scandal hits."

He nodded solemnly. "Ma'am, we're already knee-deep in scandal. I'm just here to build a paper bridge outta it."

She stared at him.

Then—bless her—opened the floodgates.


Within fifteen minutes, Tyrone had unearthed:

- A janitor paid triple scale for "ghost cleaning services" at a school that closed in 2009.

- Textbooks billed twice—and still never delivered.

- A consulting firm called *EduVantaSolutions* paid $400,000 for "curriculum strategy," which turned out to be a recycled PowerPoint and a blurry JPEG of a triangle labeled "Learning."

But the real find?

**The Red Binder.**


It was tucked in the back, behind a stack of forgotten district lunch menus.

Inside: forged invoices, missing W-2s, and payment authorizations linked to a shady donor from Cinnamon Belle's PAC—**Kenneth "Kenny D" Dawson.**

A local contractor.

And Cinnamon's former situationship.

Tyrone flipped a page.

There it was.

**$75K for "Education Innovation Consulting" billed three days after a campaign brunch.** No work. No deliverables. Just a signed approval from the now-mysteriously-resigned School Board Chair.


Tyrone stood up slowly, red binder under arm like it was nuclear material.

He turned to LaThonda.

"You ever seen anything like this?"

She nodded.

"Yep. But nobody ever asked the right questions before."

"Who's the one person who'd try to bury this?"

LaThonda leaned in, voice low.

"You ain't heard this from me, but… check Pastor Ricky's foundation. The 'youth outreach' program? That's the piggy bank."

Tyrone blinked.

"And here I thought he just hated gay books and drumlines."


He walked out of the records office like a man who'd just touched the wire.

Binder tight in hand.

Phone buzzing.

Text from Nana:
**"Bring whatever you find. We're gonna light this town up with it."**

Tyrone grinned.

"Time to audit a few souls."


**The Pastor Pushback**

**POV: Nana May Jackson**
**Setting: Glory & Dominion Mega-Tabernacle – Sunday Morning Service**

The church parking lot looked like the county fair and a car dealership had a baby.

Luxury SUVs. Shiny hats. Sinners in stilettos. The choir's robes were crisp. The A/C inside could freeze a demon.

**Pastor Ricky's** voice boomed through the sound system like God had a Bluetooth mic.

"...and now we got folks in positions of power who think morality can be replaced with popularity!"

The congregation murmured. **"Amen!"** and **"Teach it, Pastor!"**

Nana stood in the back. Alone. No entourage. Just her cane, her pearls, and a folder thick with divine vengeance.

She waited.

Like judgment.


Pastor Ricky wiped his brow. "We must pray for our town! Pray for our leadership! Because *somebody* out there thinks just because you got a few votes and a fancy livestream, you got the right to tear down the Lord's house!"

The crowd hollered.

"See, we got women out here with dirty secrets," he continued. "Women with *past lives*, takin' up the mantle of government like they pure as Moses' sandals!"

Nana stepped forward.

He saw her.

His lips twitched.

The choir kept playing.

Bad idea.


Nana walked up the center aisle like a courtroom prosecutor dressed by QVC.

People parted like they remembered she'd once put a racist principal in a neck brace and still made it to Bible study.

She climbed the steps of the pulpit.

Didn't ask.

Just took the mic.


**"Thank you, Pastor,"** she said, cool as shade on a July grave. "Now let's talk about the *real sermon.*"

A hush fell. A baby stopped crying. An usher's wig trembled.

Nana opened the folder.

Held up a color copy.

It was a check.

Made out from **"Glory & Dominion Youth Fund"** to a luxury resort in Atlanta. Memo line: *"Leadership retreat."*

Then another.

$12,000 in "motivation fees" paid to Pastor Ricky's niece… who lived in Bermuda.

Then another.

"Education Initiative Honorarium" deposited directly into an account shared by **Kenny D Dawson.**

She flipped the mic in her hand like a baton.

"Now, I'm just a woman with a cane and a conscience," she said. "But it seems to me the man yelling about morality should maybe explain why the church budget got more private jets than Bibles."

Gasps.

One deacon fainted.

A choir member muttered, "Not *again.*"

**Pastor Ricky stepped forward, voice warbling. "Now wait just a—"**

"No," Nana said, voice steel. "You called me a snake in sheep's clothing. But I'm not hiding. I'm here. *With names. With numbers.* You want a fight? God says bring witnesses. I brought notarized ones."

Someone yelled from the pews, "EXPOSE HIM!"

Another: "WE BEEN GIVIN' TITHES TO FRAUD!"

**Nana turned to the crowd.**

"I'm not asking you to stop worshipping. I'm asking you to *start investigating.* Your faith don't need to be blind. Just bold."

She handed the folder to an usher.

Turned.

And walked out as the sanctuary erupted in confusion, shouting, and the sound of spiritual house-cleaning.

**Outside, Ronny waited by the car.**

"You just burned down the tabernacle, didn't you?"

Nana got in, shut the door.

"Just fumigated it."

**The Midnight Offer**

**POV: Nana May Jackson**
**Setting: Nana's Front Porch – Just After Midnight**

The porch light was still on.

Nana rocked slowly in her chair, sweet tea in hand, slippers on, cane nearby. Not asleep. Not tired.

*Waiting.*

The stars blinked like nosy neighbors. Crickets performed backup. Somewhere, a possum was plotting in the trash cans. Classic Dusty Springs ambiance.

Then the black sedan pulled up.

Right on cue.

The man who stepped out wore a suit that cost more than most rent. **Slick. Pale. Unnamed.** The kind of guy who didn't do introductions—just transactions.

He approached with a confident smirk and a folder that definitely didn't contain banana bread recipes.

"Ms. Jackson," he said.

"You're late," she replied. "Figured bribery shows up by 10:30."

He chuckled. "I represent a group of concerned investors."

"Lemme guess. Developers who hate zoning laws. Tech bros with fake nonprofits. Or maybe folks who miss the good ol' days when corruption had manners?"

He offered the folder.

Inside:

- A check. Seven figures.

- A pre-written resignation letter.

- A seat on the board of something called *The Prosperity Collective.*

**Nana didn't blink.**

"You tryin' to buy me out of my own house with hush money and LinkedIn fluff?"

"It's a win-win," the man said. "You retire gracefully. We bring 'progress' to Dusty Springs. You walk away wealthy. Respected. Protected."

She took the check. Examined it like it was a cockroach.

Then tore it in half.

And again.

And again.

Until she dropped the confetti on the porch between them like ashes.

"You ever been slapped with a cast-iron skillet?" she asked, her voice velvet and venom.

"No."

"Then I suggest you *get back in your car* and drive your vulture behind back to whatever tax haven spawned you."

He didn't move.

She leaned forward.

"You think power comes from money. I've got *pictures,* sugar. Videos. Testimonies. Backups. And a livestream button on this phone that could set your world on fire by breakfast."

She smiled.

"And unlike y'all, I don't bluff."

**The man hesitated.**

Then—wisely—turned, got back into the car, and drove away.

No words. No threats.

Just retreat.

Nana sipped her tea.

"Thought so."

From inside the house, Velma peeked out through the curtain.

"Who was that?"

"Ghost of Jim Crow Past."

"Bringin' envelopes again?"

"More like kindling."

They both laughed. Softly. But with teeth.

## The Youth Uprising

**POV: Bliss (formerly Cinnamon's campaign intern, now Gen Z civic savage)**
**Setting: Dusty Springs High School Gym – Evening Youth Forum**

The gym smelled like disinfectant and old victories.

Folded bleachers. Dusty banners. The scoreboard stuck at 44-44 like the universe wanted balance.

Bliss stood near the center of the makeshift stage, flanked by a volunteer DJ, a student photographer, and a box of off-brand granola bars labeled *"SnackUp."*

She tapped the mic.

Feedback. Classic.

Then:
"Alright. Welcome to the first-ever Dusty Springs Youth Power Assembly. If you're over thirty, don't worry—we brought a translator."

Scattered laughter.

She grinned. "This ain't about respectability politics. This is about *reality politics.*"

**The crowd was a glorious Gen Z chaos collage:**

- Hoodies over protest shirts.
- Glitter eyeliner next to Malcolm X pins.
- Teens live-streaming on three platforms.
- Two kids making protest signs out of their math homework.

They weren't here for a civics lesson.

They *were* the civics lesson.

**Bliss gestured behind her to a giant poster:**
*"We Don't Want a Seat. We Want to Flip the Table."*

She nodded to the crowd.
"What do *you* need from your city?"

Hands shot up. Voices came fast.

- "Mental health counselors who aren't just attendance police."
- "More than one queer-friendly safe space that isn't a broom closet behind the nurse's office."
- "Free Wi-Fi that actually *works* so we can do homework without stealing it from Starbucks."
- "No more cops at school—bring back art and music instead."

**Bliss captured every word on the whiteboard.**

Then, from the back, a voice rang out:

"She's just pandering for Nana's campaign."

Heads turned. Tension built.

Bliss didn't flinch.

"I quit Cinnamon's team when I realized performative politics wasn't the same as public service. I don't want power. I want systems that *don't collapse every time we ask to be heard.*"

A few claps.

Then more.

Then a standing ovation from the *students.*


And then… Nana entered.

Quiet.

Alone.

Unannounced.

Bliss blinked, surprised.

The room hushed. Phones turned. Someone whispered, "Is that *her*?"

Nana walked straight up to the mic.

Paused.

Then:
"I ain't here to speak. I'm here to *listen.* Carry on."

She stepped to the back of the gym and sat on a metal folding chair like a grandmother at a recital.

Bliss's voice cracked just a little.
"Okay then. Let's write our demands."


An hour passed. Then two.

And by the end, they had:

- A Youth City Council proposal.

- A plan for participatory budgeting.

- A monthly forum schedule with livestreams and anonymous submissions.

And a movement.

Nana walked up as the forum ended.

"You did good, baby."

Bliss smiled.

"So did you."

Nana nodded. "The future don't need saving. It just needs space."


**The Ordinance of Reckoning**

**POV: Nana May Jackson**
**Setting: Dusty Springs City Council Chambers – Live Session**

The chamber looked like every bad civic dream come to life.

Wood paneling. Fluorescent lights. A half-working mic system that made every voice sound like a haunted CB radio.

The audience seats were full: church folks in their Sunday best, local teachers holding signs, young people with dyed hair and clipboards, and Barbara Cain in a cheetah-print pantsuit trying to pretend she wasn't sweating through her foundation.

Nana sat center stage, gavel in front of her like Thor's retired cousin.

To her right: Councilman Edgar Price, now visibly thinner since she'd started issuing subpoenas like party favors.

To her left: Quita, newly appointed ethics officer, dressed like she just came from church and court and was ready to win both.

Nana tapped the mic.

"Let's call this meeting to order before the Lord returns and finds us still negotiating morality."

The crowd laughed.

Edgar winced.

**Nana rose.**

"Today, I submit for vote the *Dusty Springs Ethical Governance and Transparency Ordinance*—a law designed to ensure that if you're gettin' paid by this city, you damn well better be earnin' it."

She listed the contents, one by one:

- Mandatory quarterly audits for every department.

- All campaign donations over $500 disclosed in public forum.

- City contracts reviewed for nepotism, kickbacks, and cousin favoritism.

- A Whistleblower Protection Office funded and staffed.

Councilman Price cleared his throat.

"This feels a little… accusatory."

Nana turned. "That's 'cause it *is.* If you ain't doin' dirt, you got nothin' to worry about. Unless guilt's just sittin' on your lap whisperin' sweet nothings."

Barbara Cain spoke next. "This will stall our development projects."

"Maybe," Nana said. "But it'll stall your corruption faster."

Someone from the audience hollered, "PREACH, AUNTIE!"

A hand shot up from the back.

Pastor Ricky.

Nana squinted.

"You ain't got a seat on this council."

"I've been invited by the Committee for Moral Oversight."

"The only committee you run is for laundering guilt and dodgin' taxes."

Gasps.

Council murmurs.

Ronny, from the corner livestreaming, whispered, "We trending, y'all. We are so trending."

**The vote was called.**

Hands raised.

Councilman Price: yes.
Barbara: no.
Three others: yes, no, abstain, yes.

The final vote fell to the tie-breaker seat—held by one **interim appointee**, recently promoted: **Velma.**

She stood slowly.

Looked around.

Then smiled.

"I didn't raise my kids to live under cowards. I vote yes."

Gavel slammed.

The ordinance passed.

Applause exploded. Nana's phone buzzed with media requests. A kid in the front row yelled, "Make her President!"

Nana sat back down, sipped her water like it was whiskey, and looked at the room of old money, young blood, and boiling resistance.

One down.

A city to go.

**[End of Chapter 10.]**

# Chapter 11: The Rebuild Ain't Quiet

**The First 48 Hours**

**POV: Nana May Jackson**
**Setting: Mayor's Office – Day One, 7:57 a.m.**

Nana stood at the threshold of the mayor's office with a jumbo mug labeled *"World's Oldest Problem."*

She sipped it like it was laced with justice and cayenne.

Behind her, Velma held a clipboard. Bliss carried a stack of digital petitions. Tyrone had already hacked the internal city server and replaced the official mayoral photo with a gif of Nana side-eying Barbara Cain.

"Y'all ready?" Nana asked.

Velma smirked. "I've been ready since 1976."


**The door creaked open.**

Inside: mahogany everything. Smelled like cologne, corruption, and entitlement. A framed portrait of Mayor Eustace hung above the desk.

Nana stared at it.

"Take it down."

Velma hesitated.

"You sure?"

"Baby," Nana said, sipping her coffee, "if I wanted to stare at failure, I'd look at my first marriage certificate."

Velma yanked it down with a satisfying *crack.*

**8:05 a.m.** – Nana fired three department heads via group Zoom. Two cried. One tried to gaslight her with jargon. She muted him and said, "You can collect your pension in decaf."

8:17 a.m. – She appointed a bilingual sanitation director, a formerly incarcerated urban planner, and a queer social worker as deputy commissioner of housing.

"Experience and receipts," Nana told the press. "Not connections and cousins."

8:34 a.m. – A reporter asked if she was concerned about backlash.

Nana blinked. "Baby, backlash is just proof you hit something worth swinging at."


**At 9:12 a.m., Pastor Ricky called.**

Nana declined the call.

He texted: "Let's be civil."

She texted back: "Let's be subpoenaed."


By lunch, she'd replaced the city's budget software with an open-access dashboard called "Where Yo' Money Went," designed by Tyrone and beta tested by his barber.

Each department had its own tab. Each tab had emoji ratings, citizen comment sections, and receipts.

The Parks Department had already received four stars and a love letter.

The Public Works Department? One broken-heart emoji and a GIF of a sinkhole swallowing a sedan.

**At 2:40 p.m., Nana held her first full-staff meeting.**

She didn't sit at the desk.

She stood in front of it like it was a pulpit and she was a prophet with a to-do list.

"This ain't a job," she said. "It's a damn restoration project. If you need comfort, go to church. If you want ease, try retail. But if you want to make history... *clock in.*"

**Someone asked what her long-term vision was.**

She didn't hesitate.

"Equity. Audacity. Accessibility. And the end of every damn lie this city used to survive."

She paused.

"Oh, and bike lanes."

**That night, as the building emptied, Nana remained.**

Alone.

She walked the perimeter of her office, dragging her fingers along the woodwork, the history, the bloodline of power passed like a bad inheritance.

She stopped at the window.

Outside, Dusty Springs was still awake.

She whispered, not to herself, but to the city.

"I'm not your queen. I'm your consequence."


**The Appointment Heard 'Round the Town**

**POV: Bliss Montoya**
**Setting: Community Hall Press Room & WQTS Local Radio (Dual Timeline)**
**Time: 11:03 a.m. & 2:25 p.m. – Day Two of Nana's Term**


Bliss adjusted her blazer in the community hall bathroom mirror and whispered to herself like a woman trying to remember if she put deodorant on both armpits.

"You're not scared. You're *qualified.* You're not scared. You're— oh God, why is my eye twitching?"

Velma knocked on the door.

"You better come on before I tell them you fainted and I had to drag your TikToking ass to the podium."


**The press room was packed.**

Reporters. Activists. Cinnamon's old donors with fake smiles and pens ready to jot down gotcha quotes. A few students from Bliss's high school government club were in the back, already live-streaming.

And at the front?

Nana.

Hair wrapped tight. Earrings like brass knuckles dipped in wisdom.

**She stepped up to the mic.**

"This town talks a big game about 'youth engagement,' but somehow, when young people actually show up, they get handed pamphlets and pizza—not *power.*"

Beat.

"Well, I don't do symbolism. I do structure."

**She turned.**

"Bliss Montoya. Step forward."

Bliss froze.

The cameras clicked like gunfire.

Velma whispered, "Move, baby. History don't wait for nerves."

**Nana continued.**

"This young woman didn't just organize voters. She built policy. She dismantled lies with facts. And she doesn't need permission to lead—just a microphone."

"She is Dusty Springs' first-ever **Youth Commissioner.** Effective immediately. Salary, voting rights, and full oversight on education, tech, and mental health initiatives."

**Gasps.**

Whispers.

A reporter stood up. "Mayor Jackson—this is highly irregular. She's 19."

Nana didn't blink.

"You know what else is irregular? A town budget that lists a pet psychic before youth services. Sit down."


Later that afternoon, Bliss sat in the *WQTS* radio booth, trying not to hyperventilate into the mic.

"...I mean, I wasn't expecting it. But I'm ready. Our generation's been told we're too emotional, too radical, too soft. But maybe it's not softness—it's just *not being numb yet.*"

The host raised an eyebrow. "You think the city's ready for you?"

Bliss smiled.

"I don't think cities get *ready.* I think they get disrupted."


**Cut to: Twitter. TikTok. Reddit.**

**#YouthCommissionerBliss**
**#MontoyaForThePeople**
**#TheTeensHaveEnteredTheChat**

And one heavily filtered meme of Bliss Photoshopped as Beyoncé holding the Constitution.


**Meanwhile, at a country club patio across town:**

Barbara Cain took a long sip of chardonnay and whispered to Cinnamon,

"If Nana starts handing out titles to teenagers, I swear I'm gonna vomit in my pearls."

Cinnamon raised her sunglasses.

"Then you better double up on pearls."


## The Ghost of Ricky Past

**POV: Velma Houston**
**Setting: State Capitol – Ethics Committee Wing / Hallway Outside Hearing Room**
**Time: Day Three of Nana's Term, 1:12 p.m.**


Velma walked down the marble corridor like she was late to an exorcism.

Clutching a leather satchel like it contained secrets—and it did.

Inside:

- A formal ethics complaint against Pastor Ricky T. Walls

- 148 pages of financial irregularities

- Whistleblower affidavits

- Two burner phone logs

- A USB marked *"The Choirboy Files"*

- And a receipt for a jet ski labeled *"Community Baptism Equipment"*

Outside the hearing room, a junior staffer tried to stop her.

"Ma'am, the committee's not taking walk-ins toda—"

Velma stopped walking.

"I am not a walk-in. I am a walk-*through.* Now move."

He moved.


Inside the hearing room, Ricky sat flanked by two lawyers in $2,000 suits and $10 souls. He wore his signature white blazer and preacher's grin—the kind that could bless or bury depending on the angle.

Velma didn't sit.

She walked to the table, pulled the mic close, and started reading:

"**Item One:** Misappropriation of state disaster relief funds for the renovation of a private guesthouse labeled 'Healing Cabin.'"

"**Item Two:** A nonprofit named *Youth For Truth,* receiving $400k annually, with no traceable programming or staffing."

"**Item Three:** A wire transfer to *Dusty Enterprises LLC* on the same day as a council vote he influenced with sermon endorsements."


**Ricky chuckled.**
"Sister Velma, I always admired your conviction. But you been nursing a grudge longer than Moses wandered."

Velma stared him down.

"Conviction is what comes *after* the trial, Ricky. And baby, I just booked you a reservation."

**The room fell silent.**

Then the chairperson asked:

"Do you have corroboration?"

Velma pulled out the USB.
"Every sin, timestamped."

**She added:**

"And you'll find an audio recording labeled *'Thursday Night Prayer Call – But Make It Criminal.'* It features our friend here discussing how many council votes it takes to cancel a grant review."

**Ricky paled.**

One of his lawyers leaned in, whispering frantically.

Velma gathered her papers.

"I'll leave y'all to digest. Call me when you're ready to schedule the revival."

**As she walked out, Ricky called after her.**

"You really think you changed anything?"

Velma paused in the doorway.

"Baby... I didn't come to change *things*. I came to change *what you call normal*."

Back in Dusty Springs, Nana got the text from Velma:

**"Delivery made. Expect legal thunder in 5-7 business days."**

Nana replied:

"Might want to put a prayer circle on backorder."


**The Exorcism of City Budget 2025**

**POV: Tyrone Dupree**
**Setting: City Council Emergency Session – Live-Streamed**
**Time: Day Four of Nana's Term, 6:30 p.m.**

Tyrone didn't wear a tie.

He wore a T-shirt that read:
**"I See Broke People (They're Hiding in City Hall)."**

He stood behind a podium that had seen more lies than a dating app inbox and plugged his laptop into the screen projector.

Behind him, Nana sat with her council. Velma had popcorn. Bliss had backup slides. The other council members looked like they'd just walked into a tech seminar and smelled a career-ending audit.

"Ladies, gentlemen, and budget leeches," Tyrone began. "I present to you: **the unholy ghost of Dusty Springs fiscal planning.**"


**Slide one:** a 3D pie chart of last year's budget.

Labeled:

- "MAYBE LEGIT"

- "SUS"

- "PASTOR RICKY'S PRIVATE AIRPORT HANGAR"

- "WTF IS THIS?"

Laughter in the chamber.

Tyrone tapped a button.

**Next slide:** A heat map of vendor payouts. One vendor—*BlessedHands Co.*—appeared 47 times. No office. No services listed. Just $312K in "consulting fees."

Tyrone paused.
"Turns out BlessedHands is registered to a post office box shared by Ricky's cousin... and his cat."


**Slide three:** Salaries of deputy mayors—*five of them,* all men, all related to previous council chairs.
One listed "emergency palm reader consultation" as an expense.

Tyrone let that one hang.

"I'll give y'all a moment to adjust your blood pressure medication."


**He pivoted.**

"This year's proposed budget? Different beast."

Slide four:

- 21% Education

- 19% Infrastructure
- 16% Housing & Mental Health
- 8% Small Biz Grants
- 5% Youth Innovation
- 0% Bullsh*t

At the bottom: **Public Ledger Access QR Code.**

Tyrone smirked.

"Citizens can now see where every dollar goes, complain in real time, and even rank department transparency with memes. Because fear of accountability hits different when there's a SpongeBob GIF next to your audit score."

**A reporter whispered, "Is this even legal?"**

Tyrone:
"No, it's *ethical.* That's why it feels so weird to y'all."

**Pastor Ricky's former budget aide tried to interrupt.**

"But this model is unsustainable! What about discretionary funds for 'rapid response initiatives'?"

Tyrone blinked.

"You mean the secret piggy bank y'all used to buy patio furniture and hush money? That's now called 'The Nope Fund.' And it's locked."

The room erupted. Some clapped. Some screamed. One aide fainted. Bliss gave him side-eye CPR.

**Nana stood. Took the mic.**

"This budget is not just a correction. It's a rebuke."

She looked at the crowd.

"Every theft you normalized? Every favor you funneled? We're calling it by name—and we're taxing it at 28%."

Velma added, "Don't worry. For y'all who miss corruption, we're setting up a museum. Donations welcome. Bribes not."

**The Letter from Cinnamon**

**POV: Nana May Jackson**
**Setting: Mayor's Office, Late Night – Day Five of Term, 10:48 p.m.**

The envelope was the color of old lipstick—deep red with gold trim and handwriting like cursive from a woman who'd once held secrets like wine: with elegance and edge.

Velma found it on the doorstep. No return address. No courier.

Just:

**To: Mayor Jackson.**
**From: A woman with nothing left to hide.**

Nana read it at her desk, alone, sipping chamomile laced with just enough bourbon to taste like victory and warning.

**"Nana—**

I lost. Fair and loud.

That night on the steps, I watched you hold a crowd without selling a damn thing. You didn't spin. You didn't smooth. You *spoke.* And for the first time in months, I remembered what it felt like to be a real woman and not a reflection in someone else's campaign ad.

So here's the truth. Not the pretty one. The **ugly receipts kind.**

Attached is a list of accounts. Off-the-books donors. Hidden PACs. Pastor Ricky's offshore fund where he stores his 'emergency morality reserves.'

You'll also find a video. I never intended to use it. Thought it was my insurance. Turns out it was my indictment.

It's from a backroom deal—April 3rd. Me, Ricky, Barbara Cain, and one developer from the industrial side. They talked about rezoning your neighborhood. Said your house was an 'acceptable casualty.' I didn't stop them. I smiled.

That's my shame. And your firepower.

Do what I couldn't. Not just win—but purge."**

**Nana leaned back.**

The city outside buzzed with post-election electricity. The kind of energy that could build something... or burn it all down.

She slid the USB into her laptop.

A window opened:
**"PLAYBACK: LAST SUPPER.mp4"**

Nana didn't hit play yet.

She stared at Cinnamon's name on the envelope.

Then whispered:

"Redemption ain't always pure. Sometimes it comes wrapped in gasoline."


Velma poked her head in.

"You good?"

Nana held up the flash drive.

"Better than good."

Then:

"Ready."


**[End of Chapter 11.]**

# Chapter 12: Scorched-Earth Sermons and Sudden Audits

**BlessedHands Unblessed**

**POV: Tyrone Dupree**
**Setting: Digital Audit Office – City Hall, Converted Filing Closet**
**Time: Day Six of Nana's Term, 8:03 a.m.**

Tyrone's "office" was technically a closet with a desk, a beanbag chair, and six monitors humming like judgment.

He preferred it that way. Less bureaucracy. More bandwidth.

On the wall behind him, he'd Sharpie'd a slogan:

**"Make Corruption Catch These Hands."**


**This morning's mission?**

**Audit the hell out of BlessedHands Co.**, the mysterious vendor that had allegedly supplied Dusty Springs with consulting, prayer candles, motivational signage, and—at one point—a $14,000 "urban morale enhancement fog machine."

Tyrone sipped his fifth Red Bull.

"Let's see what Jesus bought on the city's dime today."


**He started with the vendor registration.**

The address? A **P.O. Box** in a strip mall that also hosted a vape shop, two pawn shops, and a karate dojo that only opened on Wednesdays.

Owner listed?

**B. Walls Enterprises.**

As in... Barbara Cain's late husband.

Dead ten years. Still submitting invoices.

"Damn. Even your corruption is undead," Tyrone muttered.

He followed the paper trail.

Each invoice looked spiritual but suspicious:

- "Sanctified Team-Building Retreat – $6,000"
- "Community Healing Mimosas – $3,200"
- "Emergency Baptismal Plumbing – $8,900"

Attached photo? A bottle of Moët in a hot tub.

**The shell companies were stacked like Russian dolls dipped in holy water.**

Tyrone created a map:

- **BlessedHands Co.** paid by the city.
- Funds transferred to **Dusty Revival Holdings.**
- Then to **Cain Legacy Trust.**
- Then—offshore.

He whispered to himself, "This ain't money laundering. This is full-blown *salvation laundering.*"

At 11:14 a.m., he compiled the first leak: a visual map, animated GIFs, audio overlays, and a blinking warning label that read:

**"PASTOR RICKY'S PULPIT TO PAYPAL PIPELINE – EXPOSED."**

He launched the upload via "Where Yo' Money Went."

Within 3 minutes, it had 12,000 views.

Within 10, it was trending under:

- **#HolyFraud**
- **#DustyLeaks**
- **#MoëtAndMorality**

**Bliss called.**

"Did you just post a gif of Pastor Ricky swimming in a baptismal pool filled with Monopoly money?"

Tyrone:
"Ma'am, that's **art.**"

As comments flooded in—ranging from "RICKY YOU AIN'T RIGHT" to "WHERE'S MY REFUND FOR THEM FAKE CANDLES"—Tyrone leaned back.

He cracked his knuckles.

"Next target: *First Heaven's emergency renovation slush fund.*"

Pause.

"And maybe... their weird Chick-fil-A expenses."

## Barbara Cain's 'Prayer' Brunch

**POV: Bliss Montoya**
**Setting: Cain Family Estate – Conservatory Room & Garden Courtyard**
**Time: Day Seven, Mid-Morning Brunch, 10:46 a.m.**

If colonialism and condescension had a baby, it would be this brunch.

The Cain estate's conservatory smelled like mimosas, overripe roses, and **generational tax evasion.**

Bliss stepped inside wearing a knockoff Chanel jacket and sunglasses she bought from a protest fundraiser. Her heels clicked like a countdown.

Barbara Cain—queen of powdered cheeks and weaponized whispers—stood at the center, entertaining a table of donors, board wives, and exactly one priest who only said grace when the cameras were rolling.


**"Bliss," Barbara purred.**
"I didn't realize our *Youth Commissioner* was invited."

Bliss smiled.
"I invited myself. I figured if I'm being dragged behind closed doors, I might as well show up dressed."

Laughter. Nervous. Thin.


Barbara motioned toward a seat.

"Join us. We were just discussing the importance of tradition in leadership. And how... some roles require more maturity than others."

235

Bliss sat.

Pulled out her phone.

"Funny you say that. I have a *very mature* message to share with the room."

She tapped the screen. A voice played. Cinnamon's.

*"Barbara orchestrated the whole thing. Told Ricky to tank Nana's rezoning plan. I went along with it because I thought I'd get the endorsement. But I was wrong. She used me. Told me Dusty Springs would never vote for a woman with 'chains in her closet.'"*

Gasps. Forks clinked. One of the old women nearly passed out into her avocado toast.

Barbara stood.

"That audio is fake. Slanderous. You're just a child who thinks politics is a popularity contest."

Bliss tilted her head.

"No, ma'am. I think politics is a mirror. And you're having a bad hair day."

She pulled out a second phone.

On it: a photo of Barbara accepting a briefcase from a developer whose construction permit had just been revoked by Nana. Date-stamped. GPS-logged. Cinnamon's final gift.

"Tell me, Barbara—did the prayer brunch fund that new pool you built *or* the hush money you funneled through BlessedHands LLC?"

Barbara's nostrils flared like she was about to sneeze privilege.

Bliss stood.

"I'd say God bless you... but I think She's busy right now *defunding your legacy.*"

As Bliss walked out, one of the younger brunch attendees caught up to her at the garden gate.

"Hey... I know we're not supposed to say it, but... that was badass."

Bliss turned, smiled.

"You should see what I do at city council meetings."

Back in her car, she texted Nana:

"Cain crumbled. Expect her on Fox News by dinner."
Nana replied: "Good. Tell her I'm allergic to fake prayers and bad wigs."

**Sunday, Bloody Sunday**

**POV: Nana May Jackson**
**Setting: First Heaven Pentecostal Church – Main Sanctuary**
**Time: Sunday Morning, 10:28 a.m.**

First Heaven smelled like secrets and Febreze.

The sanctuary was packed. Easter-level packed. Half the town showed up—not for salvation, but spectacle. The other half was watching the livestream, clutching popcorn and bibles like they were about to witness spiritual demolition in real time.

Pastor Ricky stood at the altar like nothing had changed.

White suit. Gold watch. Smile like he swallowed the offering plate.

Behind him: a choir swaying offbeat. Behind *them*: the trembling remnants of a legacy built on **God and grift.**


## Nana entered through the side aisle.

She didn't wear a church hat today.

She wore her mayoral badge.

And a look that said *"I came here to finish something you should've never started."*


## Ricky spotted her.

"And look who walks among us today," he said, voice smooth as buttered lies. "Our esteemed new mayor. Come to kneel before the Lord, I assume?"

Nana walked straight down the aisle.

Not kneeling. Not blinking.

She reached the front row. Turned around. Faced the crowd.

Spoke without a mic. Didn't need one.

**"I came to bear witness.**
To everything you've done in the name of God, greed, and grant money.
To every lie wrapped in scripture.
To every woman you dismissed. Every child you failed.
To every dollar laundered through *this* pulpit."

Gasps. Rustling. One choir member stopped clapping. Another fainted into a tambourine.

**Ricky tried to pivot. "Sister Nana, I don't think this is the place for political—"**

She cut him off.

"Oh, it's exactly the place. Since this is where you built your empire of bullshit and baptized it in respectability."

She pulled out a folder.

Unclipped a stack of notarized files.

"This is a breakdown of every improper financial transaction connected to your name.
Including slush funds, fake charity events, and a 'youth outreach' cruise that never left port."

**At that moment, two men in suits stepped into the sanctuary.**

Not ushers.

Federal agents.

Badges out. Walking like thunder with subpoenas.

**Ricky stuttered.**

"This is a church! You can't arrest a man during God's service!"

Agent #1: "We're not interrupting. *She's* the one preaching."


**The choir tried to sing again.**

Nana held up her hand.

Silence.

Then:

"Dusty Springs will not worship false prophets.
We will not tithe to tyranny.
And we damn sure won't let the pulpit become a laundromat."


**They cuffed Ricky mid-hymn.**

The congregation didn't cheer.
They didn't cry.
They **exhaled.**

Like they'd been holding their breath for a decade.


**Nana turned to the congregation one last time.**

"Service is dismissed. Go in truth. Go in power. And if any of y'all donated to BlessedHands, you might wanna call your banks."


**As she exited, her phone buzzed.**

Text from Tyrone:
"Budget audit just triggered an alert on Cain's slush fund. Ready for round two?"

Nana replied:

"Start the clock."


**Dusty Springs: The Docuseries**

**POV: Velma Houston**
**Setting: Community Media Center – Editing Bay & Town Hall Screening Room**
**Time: Sunday Evening, 8:49 p.m.**

Velma's voiceover was sharp enough to shave with.

"This is a story of holy men with dirty pockets. Of developer deals scribbled on prayer napkins.
Of a town that got tired of asking for justice and decided to make it… downloadable."

Onscreen, the opening credits rolled:
***"Dusty Springs: A Town Called Out" – Episode One***

Produced by the Dusty Media Collective. Narrated by Velma Houston. Edited by three pissed-off teenagers with Adobe Premiere, cracked caffeine habits, and zero fear of litigation.


**The footage wasn't blurry.**

It was surgical.

- Cinnamon's confession, voice clear as crystal.

- Ricky's budget sermons side-by-side with IRS filings.

- Barbara Cain whispering into a microphone thinking it was off. Spoiler: It wasn't.

**Cut to:** The developers laughing in a hot tub about "rezoning the coloreds."

Then: A drone shot of the neighborhood they bulldozed anyway.

Then: Nana's speech from First Heaven, overdubbed with slow-motion of Ricky getting cuffed while "Amazing Grace (Trap Remix)" played in the background.

Inside the screening room at Town Hall, the chairs were packed.

Council members. Activists. Families. Even a few of the guilty, trying to act like this was a *learning opportunity* and not an indictment.

Velma stood in the back, arms crossed, watching faces like she was taking attendance for *who still had a conscience.*

One woman wept. One man left. Another started a GoFundMe for "Legal Defense Against Cancel Culture." (It didn't crack $12.)

**Bliss leaned in during the final credits.**

"You think we went too far?"

Velma sipped her Diet Coke.

"Baby, *truth ain't ever too far.* But corruption sure knows how to overstay its welcome."

The post-credits scene? Tyrone reading budget line items like slam poetry at an open mic.

"Line 403B: $900 for 'anointed foot massages'—I call that *toes of betrayal.*
Line 665: $700 to remove lipstick from security footage—too late, *we already saw yo' sins in high def.*"

**The next morning, the docuseries had 1.2 million views.**

Trending tags:

- #DustyLeaks
- #ExorciseTheEstablishment
- #SaintsAndSubpoenas
- #NetflixNeedsToCallVelma

**Nana's inbox filled with offers:**

- Speaking engagements.
- Book deals.
- One Netflix exec asking if they could "reimagine it with zombies."

She replied:

"Already got 'em. They just wore robes."

**The Preacher, the Condos, and the Clink**

**POV: Nana May Jackson**
**Setting: State Hearing Committee – Judiciary Review Room**
**Time: Monday Morning, 9:00 a.m.**

**The room smelled like expensive soap and bad alibis.**

State senators perched on a dais like birds of prey in silk ties.
Legal teams buzzed around like flies circling fresh guilt.
And at the center: **Ricky T. Walls**, former spiritual advisor,
current defendant, future inmate.

He still wore white.

But his collar was askew.
His confidence cracked.
And his Bible? Closed.

**Nana entered wearing Dusty Springs blue and a pin that read:**

*"Transparency Is My Love Language."*

She walked past Ricky. Didn't speak.
Didn't need to.

She had already spoken volumes—in subpoenas, in
spreadsheets, and in systems reclaimed.

**Chairwoman Delgado began.**

"Madam Mayor. You've submitted over 500 pages of evidence,
including financial audits, sworn affidavits, and video testimony.
Are you prepared to offer final commentary before sentencing
recommendation?"

Nana adjusted the mic like she was tuning an instrument of truth.

**"Yes.**

This man built a kingdom on desperation.
Preached humility while billing God for steak dinners.
Hid behind scripture while rewriting our city budget like it was a damn loot box.

He rezoned affordable housing into luxury condos and called it 'revitalization.'
He told single mothers to pray harder while cashing checks from lobbyists.

And the worst part?
He made people believe **this was normal.** That justice was naïve. That righteousness was for suckers."

She paused.

"Well, *I'm not a sucker.* I'm the Mayor."

**Ricky tried to interrupt.**

"She's on a vendetta! This is a spiritual attack!"

Chairwoman Delgado banged the gavel.

"Sir, this isn't Sunday service. This is secular judgment."

**One by one, Nana presented:**

- The offshore condo holding contracts.
- The forged invoices for prayer retreats.

245

- The leaked Zoom call where Ricky called his own congregation "ATM machines with halos."

One senator gagged.

Another whispered, "We gonna need a whole *exorcism department* after this."

**Final vote: Unanimous.**

All funds frozen.
All city contracts voided.
All charges referred to state prosecutors.

Ricky collapsed into his chair like a man who finally saw the altar for what it really was: *a stage.*

As security escorted him out, he yelled back, voice breaking:

"You can take my title—but you'll never take my followers!"

From the gallery, someone shouted:

"They already unfollowed, bruh!"

Laughter. Relief. Applause.

**Nana turned to the crowd.**

"This isn't vengeance.
This is realignment.
Because from now on, the only thing holy in Dusty Springs...

Is the truth."

**As she exited the courthouse, press swarmed.**

She gave one quote.

"Today, we buried an empire of lies. Tomorrow? We build a city that doesn't need prophets—just honest people with clipboards."


**The Hum of the Engine**

**POV: Nana May Jackson**

**Setting: Nana's Kitchen, Late at Night**

The war room was quiet for the first time in days. The only sounds were the low hum of Tyrone's laptop and the soft click of Velma's knitting needles from the living room. The air, which had crackled with the energy of takedowns and subpoenas, had finally settled, thick with the scent of stale coffee and exhaustion.

Nana watched from her recliner, pretending to be asleep.

Tyrone sat at the kitchen table, the blue light of the screen casting long shadows on his face. He wasn't typing. He was just staring at lines of code for the new budget transparency app, his shoulders slumped. He had the hollowed-out look of a soldier who had won the war but hadn't yet processed the cost.

Quita entered from the hallway, not with her usual whirlwind energy, but with a quiet shuffle. She placed a plate of leftover pot roast and a glass of sweet tea next to his laptop.

"The engine can run for five minutes without you," she said softly, nudging the plate closer to him. "Eat."

Tyrone looked up, his eyes glassy with fatigue. "Just running diagnostics. Can't let it crash."

"It won't crash," Quita insisted, her voice gentle but firm. "But you will. We just buried an entire political dynasty in a week. Your brain needs carbs and your spirit needs rest."

He looked from her to the plate, then back to the screen. For a moment, he seemed ready to argue, to insist he had to keep pushing. Then, with a slow, heavy exhale, he nodded. He picked up the fork.

Nana watched them from the dim light of the living room, a deep ache and a profound pride blooming in her chest. This was the part they never showed on the news. Not the victory speeches or the dramatic arrests, but the quiet moments after. The tending to. The soft work of putting each other back together after breaking the world apart.

This, she thought, is the real infrastructure. The part that holds everything else up.

She closed her eyes, letting the quiet hum of the house settle around her. The engine was running. And for tonight, that was enough.

---

**[End of Chapter 12].**

# Chapter 13: The Resurrection of Dusty Springs

**The Blueprint Gospel**

**POV: Nana May Jackson**
**Setting: Reclaimed Construction Site – Corner of Mercy & MLK Blvd**
**Time: Thursday Morning, 9:17 a.m.**

**They used to call this corner "The Devil's Fork."**

Two liquor stores. A payday loan shack. A church that hadn't held service since Bush left office—and not the good one.

Now? Bulldozers lined the curb like metallic saints ready for battle. A stage stood where Ricky's old campaign billboard once leaned—burned out, rained on, faded like his relevance.

Nana stood centerstage in a cobalt-blue construction vest, steel-toed boots, and a mic clipped to her collar.

Behind her: blueprints. Real ones. Rolled up, detailed, stamped. Not dreams. **Deadlines.**

**The press circled.**

The town watched.

The livestream numbers ticked up: 4,000, 7,200, 10,000...

**Nana cleared her throat.**

"We've talked about what was broken.
Now let's talk about what we build.
Not from scratch.
From scars."


**She raised a clicker. A massive display unfolded.**

**Slide 1:**
**THE DUSTY SPRINGS RECLAMATION PLAN**
– 12 community-owned housing units
– 4 cooperative-run grocery stores
– Mental health urgent care with no police presence
– Civic tech incubators for youth
– A sanctuary school for displaced students


**"This is not charity.**
**This is not a facelift.**
**This is repair.**
**This is return.**
**This is what happens when justice survives long enough to put on a damn hard hat."**


**She gestured behind her. Bulldozers revved. Cranes rose.**

The crowd gasped as an old sign from Ricky's former campaign office was plucked off the building and tossed like symbolic trash into a waiting dump truck.


"The money we reclaimed from BlessedHands?
It's in these bricks.
The PACs we disbanded?

Their budgets now fund after-school tech programs.
And for every lie we burned, we're planting a tree—with receipts stapled to the roots."

## A reporter raised a hand.

"Mayor Jackson—critics say this is symbolic. That you're focusing too much on spectacle."

Nana grinned.

"Spectacle is what they call *visible progress* when they didn't get to take credit for it."

## She pointed to the crowd.

"There's nothing more radical than a Black grandma with a clipboard and a building permit."

## Applause.

Velma nodded from the back.

Tyrone live-streamed from three angles at once. Bliss tossed a muffin into the crowd like Oprah with carbs.

## Nana finished strong.

"We didn't just survive corruption.
We sued it.
We shamed it.
And now we're building a city where *they* would've never been allowed to rent.

Welcome to the resurrection."


## The Reparations Bake Sale

**POV: Bliss Montoya**
**Setting: Dusty Springs High School Front Lawn + Town Hall Plaza**
**Time: Friday Afternoon, 4:00 p.m. – Sunset**


There were cupcakes shaped like ballot boxes.
Sugar cookies frosted with the words "DEFUND DECEPTION."
And a four-tiered red velvet cake shaped like Barbara Cain's old house—already missing a wing.

Welcome to the **first annual Reparations Bake Sale.**

Bliss didn't invent the idea. She just weaponized it.


What started as a fundraiser for after-school programs had become a full-blown media circus.

CNN was on-site. Local news argued over who could say "reparations" on-air without a viewer boycott.

And the menu?

- **Justice Jalapeño Cornbread**

- **Reverse-Redevelopment Pecan Pie**

- **Sweet Potato Woke Muffins**

The lemon bars? Labeled *"These Used to Be Property Lines."*

**Bliss stood in the center wearing a T-shirt that read:**

*"Pay Black Women. Or Pay Consequences."*

She grinned at the passing council members trying to pretend they were here in solidarity and not surveillance.


**A rich donor approached.**

"Is this... satire? Or... policy?"

Bliss blinked.

"It's both, Susan. We're selling muffins to fund what your taxes should've paid for in the first place."


Behind her, a student DJ blasted remixed town hall speeches over lo-fi beats. Tyrone added QR codes to every cookie box that linked to articles on historical redlining and misappropriated school budgets.

Velma live-podcasted the entire event while standing under a sign that read:

**"Eat a Scone, Learn a System."**


At 5:17 p.m., Bliss took the mic from the bake sale podium.

"They told us change takes time.

We told them we were out of time.

So, we baked change into every damn brownie.

You want to fix equity? Start with what got eaten first—our futures. Our neighborhoods. Our legacies."

The crowd erupted.

Even the old-school church ladies from Nana's district were buying "Gentrification Gummies" and asking for seconds.

At sunset, Bliss counted the total donations:

**$42,735.38**

From baked goods.

And guilt.

She texted Nana:
"School tech program now fully funded. Also, Susan Cain just Venmo'd me $10k and asked if it absolves her. I told her it's a down payment."

## Tyrone's Truth Engine Goes Public

**POV: Tyrone Dupree**
**Setting: Dusty Springs Civic Tech Festival – Town Hall Auditorium**
**Time: Saturday Morning, 10:42 a.m.**

If Edward Snowden and Wakanda had a baby, it would look like this launch.

Tyrone stood behind a podium made of recycled server towers. The stage was lit in blue and gold.
The crowd? A mashup of tech geeks, school kids, librarians, rogue auditors, and at least one ex–city accountant in a disguise.

254

Overhead, a banner read:

**"Introducing: TRUTH ENGINE BETA – Version 1.0.1 'Nana Protocol'"**

Tyrone cleared his throat and tapped the mic.

"Let's skip the fake humility. I didn't build this out of hope.
I built this out of rage.

Because watching Pastor Ricky expense $800 worth of body oils while a whole block lost power in July?
That'll make you learn Python *real quick*."

**A monitor behind him blinked on.**

**truthengine.dustysprings.gov**

➤ LIVE EXPENSE TRACKING
➤ PROPERTY DEVELOPMENT ALERTS
➤ EARMARK TRANSPARENCY DASHBOARDS
➤ "WHO BOUGHT THAT BULLSH*T?" FEATURE
➤ Complaint Uploads, Whistleblower Shield, and Historical Scandal Archive

**He clicked a demo.**

The crowd gasped.

Each data point was clickable.
Each contract was mapped.
Each shady real estate purchase glowed like a radioactive lie.

Even Barbara Cain's birthday yacht appeared under the tag "Excessive Celebrations – Unaccounted Budget."

Tyrone smirked.

"This ain't just for you to know what they bought.
It's for you to know **who paid for it.**
Spoiler: it was always you."

He introduced the whistleblower mode—**coded "CINNAMON CLASSIFIED"**—which masked identities, timestamped submissions, and auto-encrypted digital evidence. Velma shouted from the back:

"WELL DAMN. Y'all made democracy sexy again."

**A teen hacker raised her hand.**

"What happens if they try to shut this down?"

Tyrone tapped a side screen.

Backups. Mirrors. Blockchain integrations.
A network of mirrored data points called "NANA-NODE," backed up in five jurisdictions.

He shrugged.

"Let them try."

By the time the crowd poured out into the civic fair, "Truth Engine" was trending in four states.

CNN headline at noon:

**"Local Town Launches App That Actually Tells You Where the Money Went—GOP Legislators Cry in Corner."**

That night, Tyrone updated the app with a new widget:

**"Lie of the Week"** – With audio clips, memes, and a five-star *BS-rating system.*

His first upload? Ricky Walls claiming he "didn't know what a 501(c)(3) was."
It got 9.8k thumbs-down and a new caption:

"Boy, You Preach With One."

**Velma and the Archive of Shame**

**POV: Velma Houston**
**Setting: Former DMV Basement – Now "Dusty Springs Public Accountability Archive"**
**Time: Sunday Morning, 11:06 a.m.**

The room still smelled like despair and old printer ink.

Velma loved it.

She had turned the old DMV basement—once home to expired laminators and bureaucratic misery—into the **Dusty Springs Public Accountability Archive** (D-SPAA, pronounced "despair," because she was *funny like that*).

Shelves were stacked with digitized files, labeled manila folders, annotated campaign flyers, and one truly cursed oil painting of Barbara Cain in pearls, mid-bribe.

At the entrance, a sign read:

**WELCOME TO THE ARCHIVE OF SHAME**
*"Because forgetting is how they keep winning."*

And beneath that:

**Funded by The Reparations Bake Sale + One Extremely Guilty Developer.**


Velma adjusted her microphone.
She wasn't just opening a museum.
She was launching her new podcast:
**"Corrupt AF: A Civic Audio Autopsy"**

"This is Episode 1:
*'You Can't Spell Pastor Without PR Stunt'* – The Ricky Walls Autopsy."


She hit record.

"He told us to pray while he drained the budget.
Told us to forgive while he expensed a Peloton under 'pastoral movement initiatives.'

But we remember.
We remember **everything.**

Because they said the devil was in the details.
And baby, we brought a flashlight."


Around her, high school interns filed evidence into labeled drawers:

- "False Nonprofits"

- "Fake Community Listening Sessions"
- "That Time Barbara Bought a Tesla with Emergency Relief Funds"

They had a VR station where residents could "walk through" the rezoning of their neighborhoods using augmented reality and passive-aggressive commentary.

One elderly man walked through the Cain Family corruption timeline and started crying.

"My grandson didn't get that scholarship. This—this is what happened."

Velma handed him tissues and a QR code.

"Forward it. Loudly."

Outside the archive, protest art covered the walls.
Tyrone projected Truth Engine dashboards onto the building at night.
And Nana sent over a memo proposing **quarterly corruption burn ceremonies.**

Velma replied:

"Only if I get to light the match."

Later, during a press interview, a reporter asked:

"Don't you worry this is divisive? That it keeps old wounds open?"

Velma smiled.

"Oh, honey—*the wound was never closed.*
We're just showing people where it bleeds.
And now we're cauterizing it with history."


## Cinnamon's Final Confession

**POV: Nana May Jackson**
**Setting: Abandoned Church – Mount Zion Missionary**
**(Condemned but Beautiful)**
**Time: Sunday Evening, 7:33 p.m.**


The stained glass was cracked.
The pews were dusty.
The Bible on the altar had two pages stuck together with what
looked like communion wine and 1986 trauma.

Nana sat in the front pew, arms folded, eyes steady.
She wasn't here for prayer.
She was here for closure.

The door creaked.

Cinnamon walked in.

No makeup. No Gucci. No entourage.
Just a manila envelope, tired eyes, and a jaw clenched like
someone bracing for holy fire.


Nana didn't stand.

"Before you speak," she said, "just know—I don't need your
apology. I need your accuracy."

Cinnamon nodded.

"I ain't come to say sorry, Nana.
I came to say *everything else.*"


She sat beside her.
The envelope landed between them like a live grenade with a notary stamp.


"Barbara Cain wasn't just running a smear campaign.
She was funneling PAC money into fake shell projects.
Said it was for 'urban renewal.'
It was for her nephews' vape shop empire and a side condo in Boca."

"The zoning bribes?
Pastor Ricky was her middleman.
Said it was for 'spiritual discernment.'
Really, it was code for *cash under the communion table.*"


Nana's face remained stone.

"Why tell me now?"

Cinnamon looked up at the fractured Jesus above the altar.

"Because she said she'd ruin me if I broke silence.
But I'm already ruined.
So I figured I'd at least get credited for the demolition."


She pulled out a flash drive.

"Everything.
Audio. Invoices. Photos.

Including a wire transfer labeled 'Consultation with the Lord – $30,000.'"

Nana blinked.

"I knew they were bold. I didn't know they were *biblically stupid.*"


Cinnamon gave a crooked smile.

"This doesn't buy me redemption.
But maybe it buys me peace.
Or at least a restraining order against karma."

Nana reached for the flash drive.

"It buys you a signed witness protection agreement and a lifelong ban from HOA meetings."

They both chuckled. Brief. Tired.


Before she left, Cinnamon said:

"If I disappear...
Barbara didn't move to Florida.
She moved into her next victim."


Nana watched her walk away, silhouette bathed in twilight through broken stained glass.

She held the envelope in her hands.

Heavy with guilt. But **heavier with proof.**

Text to Velma:

"New drop incoming. You're gonna need a whole new folder. Label it: Divine Dirt."


**[End of Chapter 13.]**

# Chapter 14: Hell Froze Over—And So Did the Developers' Bank Accounts

**Code Red: The Permits Get Pulled**

**POV: Nana May Jackson**
**Setting: City Planning Department Headquarters – Permit Vault and Oversight Room**
**Time: Monday Morning, 9:02 a.m.**

The City Planning building always smelled like stale coffee and compromise.

Not today.

Today it smelled like toner, cold vengeance, and *accountability so thick you could file it alphabetically.*

Nana strode through the metal detectors flanked by Bliss and a local bailiff who looked like he'd just finished watching **Erin Brockovich** on repeat.

She wasn't there for a meeting.
She was there for **a municipal exorcism.**

Behind her, Velma held up her phone. Livestream on.
Hashtag: **#PermitPurgeParty**

Nana slapped a stack of color-coded folders onto the Planning Director's desk.

"See these?" she said. "These are permits tied to fraud, bribery, and enough environmental violations to give Greta Thunberg a nervous breakdown."

The Planning Director blinked.

"I—Mayor Jackson, some of these are still under review—"

She raised one eyebrow.

"Good. Cancel them before they become *evidence.*"

One by one, she called them out:

- **Cain Family Holdings #4038:** Condos named "Divine Heights" (zoned on a floodplain).

- **BlessedHands Outreach Lot D:** Meant to be a "soup kitchen," actually a developer's backdoor laundromat.

- **Righteous Real Estate LLC:** Five permits for churches that never got built but got appraised anyway.

She looked straight into Velma's camera.

"Citizens of Dusty Springs—these permits were awarded without oversight, reviewed without conscience, and used without consequence. Until now."

She turned to the permit clerk.

"Mark them revoked. Effective immediately. Digital copies deleted. Physical copies..."

She snapped her fingers.
Tyrone handed her a portable shredder and a Bluetooth speaker.

The **Imperial March** blared softly as one permit after another disappeared into the jaws of justice.

Bliss whispered, "This is petty."

Nana grinned. "No, baby. *This is policy.*"

A crowd gathered outside the glass walls.
Employees clapped. One guy cried.
Another shouted, "DO 'HOLY HEIGHTS OF HARMONY' NEXT!"

Nana obliged.

By 10:12 a.m., over **28 fraudulent permits** were officially revoked.

The Planning Department's public web portal auto-updated: **"REVOKED: Pending Legal Review / Fraudulent Activity Detected"**

Every developer tied to the Cain-Walls Axis got a courtesy email titled:

**"Your Application Has Been Smote."**

Before leaving, Nana looked back at the stunned Planning Director.

"Don't worry. You're not fired. Yet. But from now on, if a pastor wants a property rezone, make sure he ain't hiding a Porsche under his pulpit."

As she walked out, the livestream ticked past **230,000 views.**

Top comment:

*"This is better than reality TV and it actually fixes stuff."*


**The Audit That Killed a Country Club**

**POV: Tyrone Dupree**
**Setting: Regional Accounting Oversight Board – Downtown Conference Auditorium**
**Time: Monday Afternoon, 2:44 p.m.**


The accounting oversight hearing looked like the least exciting episode of C-SPAN ever filmed.
Until Tyrone hit "Play."

He and Bliss stood before a panel of forensic accountants and state tax compliance officers in a room that smelled like ink toner, bitter coffee, and repressed outrage.

Behind them, a 70-inch screen flickered to life.

Title Slide:
**DUSTY PINES COUNTRY CLUB: A CASE STUDY IN NONPROFIT DELUSION**

Subtitle:
**"Somehow God's Money Always Bought Scotch"**


Bliss took the mic first.

"Good afternoon. If you've ever wondered how a 'nonprofit country club' managed to file for tax-exempt status while also buying 400 bottles of Macallan 18 and five golf carts customized with monograms… buckle up."

Tyrone clicked through the first slide:

✗ "Charitable Mission Statement: Golf Therapy for At-Risk Youth"
✓ Actual Use: Closed Membership for Wealthy Donors, No Youth Programs Logged Since 2006

Next slide:

✗ Claimed Expenses: Pastoral Retreat
✓ Actual Expense: 3-Day Poker Tournament in Cancun, Hosted by Pastor Ricky Walls

Next slide:

✗ Claimed Facilities Repair
✓ Actual Expense: A private steam room with "Cain Cain Sugarcane" embroidered towels

A gasp rippled through the room.

Bliss chimed in.

"They wrote off caviar as *'spiritual sustenance.'*
They paid landscapers $80,000 a year to keep minorities off the tennis court."

The auditors began scribbling furiously.

One raised a hand, barely concealing a smirk.

"Where did you obtain these records?"

Tyrone smirked right back.

"We used the Pastor's own accounting software. Turns out God doesn't believe in two-factor authentication."


Final Slide:

**FRAUD ESTIMATED: $2.9 MILLION**
**TAX LIABILITY: $850,000 + Penalties**
**RECOMMENDATION: Immediate Revocation of Nonprofit Status & Full Civil Audit**


A vote was taken.
**Unanimous.**

The Chairperson leaned into the mic.

"Effective immediately, Dusty Pines Country Club loses its tax-exempt status, is referred for criminal investigation, and shall be required to return all misappropriated funds or surrender property."


A new motion passed:
The club would be repurposed as a **Civic Equity and Recreation Center**—free to the public.

Working title:

**"Justice Greens: Where Everybody Gets a Damn Tee Time."**

Tyrone and Bliss walked out to a slow clap.

Outside, news vans already waited.
Velma's podcast was queued up.
The club's ex-chairman collapsed into a folding chair muttering, "But we prayed over the scotch…"


Bliss whispered to Tyrone:

"One more down. Two snakes left to defang."

Tyrone replied, "Let's go freeze Barbara's empire."


**Barbara's Frozen Assets and Melted Dignity**

**POV: Velma Houston**
**Setting: Civil Asset Forfeiture Courtroom – 9th Circuit Courthouse**
**Time: Tuesday Morning, 8:58 a.m.**


Barbara Cain entered in designer shades and a bad attitude, flanked by two lawyers who looked like they billed by the syllable.

Velma wore flats, a neutral blouse, and a smile that could slice marble.

The courtroom was packed.
The press gallery buzzed.
Tyrone livestreamed the event under the caption:

**"Today's Forecast: Heavy Seizures with a 100% Chance of Justice."**

Judge Hightower entered, heavy with presence and heavier with receipts.

"This hearing regards the civil forfeiture of assets obtained through fraudulent nonprofit entities, political laundering, and tax code manipulation by Mrs. Barbara Alexandria Cain."

Barbara tried to smirk.
Velma took the stand.


She opened a brown leather folder.

"Your Honor, I submit into evidence 44 instances of fraudulent expense reporting, 12 shell LLCs used to hide campaign donations, 6 offshore accounts traced back to Cain Family Holdings, and one truly appalling attempt to deduct a Peloton under 'youth outreach.'"

The courtroom chuckled. Even the stenographer smirked.


Velma continued.

"The defendant claimed charity work while commissioning marble floors for her powder room.
She wrote sermons on 'sacrifice' from a $6,000 chaise lounge.
She spent public redevelopment funds on a Chanel addiction that deserves its own DSM code."


Barbara's lawyer stood.

"Objection. This is character assassination."

Judge Hightower raised an eyebrow.

272

"Counselor, you're not supposed to object when the character killed itself."


Velma laid down the deathblow:

"Your Honor, we also recovered a digital ledger labeled **'God's Work 📿'** that includes line items such as:

- 'Brunch with lobbyist – $340'

- 'Silence fee (Cinnamon) – $25,000'

- 'Faux miracle PR campaign – $7,400'

- 'Fake charity gala featuring Pitbull impersonator – $12,000'"

She held up Cinnamon's notarized statement.

"And we have a signed confession confirming it all."


Barbara's mouth dropped.
Her lawyer whispered something.
She stood.

"This is political theater."

Velma leaned in.

"Oh no, Barbara. This is **accounting revenge.**"


Judge Hightower banged the gavel.

"Effective immediately, the court hereby freezes all accounts associated with the Cain Family Trust, forfeits the properties listed under fraudulent acquisition, and refers this case to criminal prosecution."

Barbara stumbled. Her heels clicked like tiny panic attacks. The bailiff handed her an itemized list of everything she now **no longer owns.**

**She turned to Velma.**

"This isn't over."

Velma replied with surgical calm.

"No. It's just **finally begun.**"

## Scene 84: Cain and Unable: When Lobbyists Lawyer Up

**POV: Nana May Jackson**
**Setting: Highrise Law Firm Lobby → Police Cruiser**
**Time: Tuesday, 12:47 p.m.**

The lobby of Calloway & Finch was engineered to feel expensive—floor-to-ceiling windows, chrome everything, and a reception desk that looked like it had a trust fund.

Barbara Cain sat perched in a gray power suit, legs crossed, phone glued to her ear like it still obeyed her.

Her smile didn't quite reach her eyes.

Nana entered, flanked by two very official-looking investigators and **Velma wearing aviators indoors like righteous judgment.**

Barbara stood.

"I assume you're here to negotiate."

Nana didn't blink.

"I'm here to witness your final delusion in 4K."


Barbara gestured toward the elevator.

"Private conference room. Off record."

Nana raised a flash drive.

"Already off script. This is what your assistant emailed us after she realized your NDA was worth about as much as a forged miracle."


Barbara's composure cracked. Just a hairline.

"You wouldn't dare go public with this."

Velma stepped forward.

"We already did. It's trending under **#CainAndUnable.**"


Barbara turned to her lawyer—some ex-fed type with a jawline and zero soul.

She whispered. He nodded.
He approached Nana with a proposal—two options typed on linen cardstock.

1. Barbara would "quietly resign from all public positions" and "make a generous donation" to the Dusty Springs Civic Fund.

2. All charges would be considered "settled through reparative community investment."

Nana skimmed it.

Then she turned it over, wrote **"LOL"** in thick Sharpie, and handed it back.

"There will be no donation.
There will be no deal.
There will only be **justice.** And maybe a Netflix docuseries."

A beat of silence.

Then the police entered.

"Barbara Alexandria Cain, you are under arrest for tax fraud, embezzlement, perjury, and seventeen counts of public deception."

Velma whispered, "We were generous. There were *twenty-one.*"

As Barbara was handcuffed, her wig tilted just slightly—like a crown on a fallen queen.

The lobby gasped. Phones came out. Nana didn't stop them.

For a split second, the defiance in her eyes wavered, replaced by the ghost of a skinny girl in a threadbare dress being laughed out of the very country club she would one day own.

She blinked, and the steel returned.

She turned one last time. "You'll regret this."

Nana stepped close enough to whisper.

"I regret not doing it sooner."

**Outside, protesters cheered.**
One held up a sign that read:

**"Cain You Not?"**

Barbara was escorted into the cruiser.

Velma posted it with the caption:

"The Lord works in transparent municipal oversight."

**Mayor Jackson's Emergency Press Conference**

**POV: Nana May Jackson
Setting: Dusty Springs City Hall Courtyard – Pop-Up
Podium + Press Barricade
Time: Tuesday, 4:17 p.m.**

**The podium had no frills.**
Just a microphone, a seal, and a folding table repurposed from
the Parks & Rec lost-and-found.

Reporters buzzed. Cameras rolled.
Every major network was livestreaming.
Even TikTok influencers were elbowing each other for the best
angle.

Nana took the mic. No notes. No teleprompter. Just the calm
fury of a woman who once delivered babies in a blackout and
still had time to bake banana bread.

**She cleared her throat. The crowd hushed.**

"Dusty Springs.

We've been lied to.
We've been robbed.
And worse—we were told it was all in the name of God, prosperity, and community.

Today, we call that what it was: *gaslighting by Gucci-wearing hypocrites.*"

**A wave of claps rippled through the courtyard.**

Nana continued:

"For too long, corruption wore a collar and carried a clipboard.

Pastor Ricky said we were saving souls while he laundered your lunch money.
Barbara Cain told you it was urban renewal, while she bulldozed your history and sold your future."

"This administration—*my administration*—has revoked 31 fraudulent permits.
We've recovered over $3 million in misused funds.
And we've begun legal proceedings that will ensure Dusty Springs never gets played by plastic prophets again."

**She raised her voice—not loud, but iron-wrapped.**

"To every resident who lost housing to a crooked zoning deal— *we see you.*

To every teacher denied supplies while a country club wrote off cigars as 'youth development'—*we hear you.*

And to every grandma, student, janitor, and bus driver who ever said, 'Something ain't right,' but got ignored:
**You were right. And we fixed it.**"


**A reporter called out:**

"Mayor Jackson—what do you say to critics calling this a political witch hunt?"

She didn't flinch.

"If this was a witch hunt, they'd be the ones holding the broomsticks.
We're just sweeping up the ashes."


**Another asked:**

"What's next for Dusty Springs?"

Nana smiled.

"Next? We rebuild. But this time, with transparency. With truth. And without giving clout to clowns in collars."


**She looked directly into the cameras.**

"Corruption is not a spiritual gift.
Fraud is not a leadership trait.
And the Lord don't cosign your luxury car lease."


**Behind her, Bliss handed out packets titled:**

279

### "Where Your Money Goes Now – A Transparent Budget Plan"

Tyrone projected the new Truth Engine stats live behind the podium.

Velma handed out "Cain't Stop Justice" cupcakes.

And Nana?

She stepped down from the podium and into the crowd.

Because some leaders **rule from stages.**
Nana? **She governs from eye level.**


**[End of Chapter 14.]**

# Chapter 15: The Great Rebuilding Begins (With a Blowtorch and a Budget)

**Blueprints and Blowtorches: Bliss's Youth Center Breaks Ground**

**POV: Bliss Monroe**
**Setting: Former Cain Holdings Parking Lot – Now Groundbreaking Site**
**Time: Wednesday, 10:07 a.m.**


The air reeked of hot asphalt and poetic justice.

Bliss stood in steel-toed boots, holding a blueprint in one hand and a crowbar in the other like **Saint Joan of Urban Renewal.**

Behind her, what used to be Cain Holdings' private parking lot was now a fenced-off construction zone buzzing with interns, student volunteers, and three grandmas with jackhammers.

One of them? Sister Velma. Wearing a hardhat that said **"TRUTH CREW"** in glitter.


The youth center wasn't going to be some soulless city-funded box with flickering lights and motivational posters from 2006.

No.

This place would have:

- A music production studio built from repurposed confession booths

- A computer lab with coding programs, VR headsets, and cybersecurity training

- A rooftop garden with aquaponics and a tiny sign that read **"B*tch, Grow Something"**


Bliss took the mic as the crowd gathered for the groundbreaking ceremony.

"They told us there wasn't enough room in the budget.
They told us the youth didn't need more space—just more rules.

But somehow Barbara Cain found enough room in the budget for a private sauna and seventeen fake charities.

So we took her land. And now we're planting freedom in it."

A local middle schooler handed her the ceremonial golden shovel.
Bliss handed it right back.

"Symbolic shovels are for photo ops.
This is a real job."

She picked up the crowbar and smashed the "Cain Holdings Reserved Parking" sign clean off its pole.
The crowd erupted. Sister Velma sprayed the fallen sign with black paint. One word:
**"REDEEMED."**


Construction crews rolled in.

No contractors with billion-dollar bids.
This was community-led.
Union-backed.
And powered by solar panels donated by **"Nuns for Infrastructure."** (Yes, that's a real thing now. Nana made it so.)


Bliss turned to a group of teens with clipboards.

"Every week, y'all vote on what goes in here. You design the programs. You choose the mural colors. This is yours. We just handle the budget and the building permits."

One teen raised her hand.
"Can we have a podcast room with beanbags and ring lights?"

Bliss grinned.

"You can have a podcast room, a sound booth, and a *narrative justice curriculum.*

Just no conspiracy TikToks, unless they're funny and involve aliens."

By 2 p.m., the old parking lot sign had been ripped out.
By 3, a new banner went up:

**FUTURE HOME OF THE DUSTY SPRINGS LIBERATION CENTER**
*Where Youth Build, Create, and Organize Like Adults Wish They Could*

Velma handed Bliss a smoothie.
"From the new co-op. The avocado's local."

Bliss sipped.
"Tastes like vengeance."

**Velma's Community Truth Archive Goes National**

**POV: Velma Houston**
**Setting: Dusty Springs Library – Now Truth Archive HQ + Mobile Studio**
**Time: Wednesday, 5:42 p.m.**

The old library still had water stains on the ceiling and a copy of *The Purpose Driven Life* duct-taped to the front desk.

But now? It also had:

- A mobile soundproof podcast booth made out of repurposed baptismal barrels

- A solar-powered scanner farm archiving documents faster than a divorce lawyer in Texas

- And a mural of Harriet Tubman holding a USB stick that said **"RUN THE FILES"**

Velma sat in her ergonomic chair (donated by a retired whistleblower) surrounded by a staff of teenage interns, retired librarians, and one sassy drag queen named Manifest Destiny who handled metadata tagging like a god.

On screen, the livestream viewer count ticked up past 100K.

Title:

**"From Dusty Springs to D.C.: How One Small Town Made the Truth Trend"**

Velma leaned into the mic.

"Tonight's story isn't about downfall.
It's about documentation.
And the paper trail that finally dragged the powerful into the sunlight."

**Behind her, volunteers uploaded:**

- Redacted contracts from Pastor Ricky's offshore charities

- Texts between Barbara Cain and her "miracle management consultant"

- Voicemails from corrupt city officials who thought "delete" meant "disappear"

What started as a Google Drive link passed around at church fish fries had now gone **national.**

Other cities were calling in:

- **Flint, Michigan** wanted to replicate the "Testify & Archive" booth

- **Jackson, Mississippi** requested the community memory training kit

- A church in **Atlanta** offered to house a satellite Truth Hub in its old choir rehearsal room

**Velma smiled like a woman who just saw karma do the splits.**

"You can't stop corruption without receipts.
You can't fix lies without a file system.
And you sure as hell can't gaslight a librarian."

**An intern buzzed in:**

"Velma, NPR's on the line. They want an interview."

She sipped her ginger tea.

"Tell NPR I'm booked, but I'll send them the receipts in alphabetical order with timestamps."

**The muralist tapped her on the shoulder.**

"Ms. Velma, we finished the outside wall. Want to see?"

Velma stepped outside.

On the brick wall, in vibrant defiant colors:

**"In Memory of Every Truth They Tried to Erase—
We Wrote It Down, B\*tch."**

She stared at it. Didn't cry. Just nodded.

"Print that on a grant application."


**Nana's Budget Bootcamp: Where Every Dollar Stands Trial**

**POV: Nana May Jackson
Setting: City Hall Auditorium – Rebranded "Civic
Courtroom for the Budget Battle"
Time: Thursday, 6:01 p.m.**


The room looked like Judge Judy and Shark Tank had a budget-conscious baby.

One side of the hall held giant foam-core printouts of line-item allocations.
The other had folding chairs for residents, each with a clicker, a ballot, and a program that read:

**"Welcome to Budget Bootcamp: Where Your Opinion Pays Dividends"**

And at the front?

Mayor Nana May Jackson.
Wearing bifocals, boots, and the expression of a woman who knew **exactly** how much a bullshit line-item for "spiritual consulting" should cost: **$0.00.**

**She addressed the crowd:**

"Today, we try the budget.
Not propose it. Not pitch it.
We put it under oath and ask:

Who do you serve?
What do you build?
And who benefits when you survive the cut?"

**A giant screen displayed a breakdown of recovered funds:**

- 💰 $3.4M in seized Cain-Walls holdings

- ☐ $890K in canceled contracts from developer grift

- 🔍 $1.2M in new state transparency grants

Total: **$5.49M in civic resurrection capital.**

**Nana invited departments to make their cases.**

**First up: Parks & Rec.**

"Requesting $400,000 for a shade structure, updated trail maps, and one community goat yoga pilot."

Nana turned to the crowd.

"Y'all want goat yoga?"

One senior in the back yelled, "If the goat's unionized!"

Clickers clicked. The screen flashed:
✓ *Approved: 91%*

**Next: Public Safety.**

Requested: $500,000.

Nana raised an eyebrow.

"For what?"

The deputy stammered. "Uh…rebranding. New uniforms. A community trust initiative?"

Nana folded her arms.

"Trust doesn't come from matching polos."

The crowd booed.
Clickers clicked.

✗ *Rejected: 76%*


Velma stood up next, presenting the **Civic Memory Preservation Fund.**

"We request $100K to hire five truth archivists and digitally scan every dusty-ass record left by Cain & Walls before they 'go missing.'"

The crowd cheered. One teen yelled, "Preserve that petty!"

✓ *Approved: 98%*


By 8 p.m., a new people-approved budget had been ratified. It was posted live to **The Truth Engine** with full visibility, line-item receipts, and a public comment section titled:

**"If You See Bullsht, Say Bullsht."**

**Nana closed the night with this:**

"For too long, money flowed like holy water—with no one asking where the well was.
From now on, every dollar answers to you."

As the crowd filed out, someone spray-painted above the City Hall entrance:

**"Accountability Lives Here Now."**

Nana didn't stop them.

**Tyrone Codes for Liberation**

**POV: Tyrone Dupree**
**Setting: Dusty Springs High School Gym – Now the Liberation Hack Lab**
**Time: Friday, 3:47 p.m.**

**The gym smelled like teenage sweat, soldering irons, and revolution.**

The basketball court was now a sea of laptops, extension cords, half-drunk Red Bulls, and one kid who had turned a discarded Alexa into a whistleblower detector.

Above the bleachers hung a banner that read:

**"Dusty Springs Hack for Liberation – No Firewalls, No Gatekeepers, No Excuses."**

Tyrone stood at center court with a dry erase marker and enough built-up energy to reboot the damn ZIP code.

Behind him, a projector displayed the first app prototype:

**RENT ARMOR**
*Anonymously reports landlord violations, sends auto-notifications to the housing board, and generates PDF demand letters.*

The room of teens, aunties, grad students, and retired postal workers erupted in applause.

Tyrone raised his hands.

"We don't beg for justice.
We build the damn infrastructure that delivers it.

This ain't Silicon Valley.
It's **Civic Code from the Streets Up.**"

Bliss entered, holding a tray of protest-themed cupcakes ("Delete System32" in frosting).

She whispered, "You're at 500 live viewers and 3 job offers."

Tyrone replied, "Make it 501. I just hired myself."

The next app?

**PublicEyes**

- Allows live recording of city officials at public events
- Automatically transcribes speeches

- Compares their statements to historical votes
- Flags hypocrisy with a flashing icon and dramatic violin music

A voice in the crowd shouted:
**"Yo! That's the Snitch App for Politicians!"**

Tyrone grinned.

"We don't snitch—we **document the contradictions.**"


**One girl raised her hand.**

"Can we build a chatbot that helps grandma fill out city grant apps?"

He nodded.

"We'll call it 'Grants for Grannies.' First version launches next week."


**By nightfall, five working apps were coded.**

- **Tenant Titan** – landlord database + rent cap tracker
- **Truth Loop** – audio-based story recording + auto-archive tool
- **PowerWatch** – real-time alerts when city council meetings try to hide agenda items
- **VoteSniff** – flags voter suppression tricks before they hit the streets
- **The B.S. Detector** – reads zoning permits aloud and screams if the math don't math

Tyrone looked around at the gym full of faces—Black, brown, queer, elder, teen, ex-cons, librarians, farm kids.

This was **not** a startup.

This was **survival coding.**

"They had AI before us, but we've always had survival protocols.

Now we put 'em in apps."

**Scene closed with a cheer:**

**"No bugs! No bribes! No billionaires!"**

Tyrone nodded, thinking:

"Give us a keyboard, and we'll deconstruct the machine."

**The Demolition Parade**

**POV: Group Ensemble (Nana, Tyrone, Bliss, Velma, and the Townies)**
**Setting: Main Street to Cain Towers – Final Site of Former Cain Holdings**
**Time: Saturday, 11:11 a.m. (because the ancestors said so)**

The town gathered in their finest:

- Bliss wore a jumpsuit made of old Cain Holdings banners—each strip now reading "Community-Owned"

- Tyrone rocked a hoodie that said **"I Came to Code and Collapse Systems"**

- Nana donned a red leather trench with a sash reading **"Mayor of These Streets"**

- Velma held the detonator remote in one hand and a hymnbook in the other

The parade began with a local drumline marching to the beat of destiny.

Then came the floats:

1. A mock-up of Barbara Cain's mansion with Monopoly money shooting out of the chimney

2. A papier-mâché of Pastor Ricky being chased by a giant tax audit

3. A 12-foot goat statue named **Accountabilitina** that pooped shredded zoning permits

Kids tossed seed bombs into vacant lots as confetti rained from drones shaped like middle fingers.

Local elders rode in restored lowriders wrapped in banners that read:

**"We Remember. We Rebuild. We Repurpose Your Bullsh*t."**

Finally, the parade reached the site of Cain Towers—former headquarters of corruption, now draped in protest art and two enormous painted words:

## "THIS SPACE IS UNDER NEW MANAGEMENT."

**Nana stepped forward with the mic.**

"This ain't just demolition.
It's liberation.

These buildings stole our skyline, our savings, and our dignity.
Now?
We get the skyline back."

**Velma handed her the detonator.**

Tyrone counted down with the crowd.

"3..."
"2..."
"1..."

BOOM.

Cain Towers crumbled like every false promise made under the Cain administration.

The crowd erupted.
Choirs sang.
Drums thundered.
One woman yelled, **"THIS IS MY JUNETEENTH NOW."**

**A cloud of dust settled.**

In its place?

A banner unfurled from a crane overhead:

**COMING SOON: The Dusty Springs Museum of Resistance, Rebirth & Ratchet Joy**

**Nana raised a fist.**

Bliss bowed her head.

Tyrone uploaded a livestream titled:

**"When the People Run the Parade *and* the Permits."**

**The final shot of the scene:**

A little girl standing on rubble, pointing to the sky, saying:

"That's where we'll build the library."

**[End of Chapter 15.]**

# Chapter 16: Redemption Ain't Free, But It's Fully Funded

**Bliss Starts the 'Reclaim & Reparent' Program**

**POV: Bliss Monroe**
**Setting: Dusty Springs Liberation Center – Basement Level, "The Healing Room"**
**Time: Sunday, 6:03 p.m.**

The room was round.
No sharp corners.
No fluorescent lights.
Just beanbags, soft pillows, one defiant lava lamp, and a whiteboard that read:

**Welcome to Reclaim & Reparent**
*No Shame. No Blame. Just Real Work and Snacks.*

Bliss adjusted the diffuser. Lavender, peppermint, and Black girl magic wafted through the space.

Seven teens shuffled in. Some looked curious.
Some looked like they'd rather be in detention.
One wore headphones over his hoodie.
Another refused to sit—until she saw the "Fuck Around and Find Growth" beanbag chair.

Bliss didn't lecture. She sat with them. Eye level.
She passed around journals with glitter pens, Sharpies, and one labeled "This Journal Is More Honest Than My Pastor."

"You don't gotta write about your trauma.
You don't even gotta call it trauma.
You can write about a song, a memory, a time you felt like disappearing."

**One boy raised his hand.**

"Why does it gotta be 'Reparent'? Ain't that sayin' my parents failed?"

Bliss nodded, slowly.

"Some of our parents did their best. Some did their worst. Some just disappeared.

This ain't about blame.
This is about **giving yourself what nobody else gave you— on purpose.**"

**The girl in the corner spoke up, voice low.**

"You ever get told you were too loud? Or too sensitive? Like… your feelings were the problem?"

Bliss raised her hand like a survivor swearing in.

"All the time. And I started believing it.
Until I learned that **being sensitive was never the issue— being ignored was.**"

**They sat in silence for a moment.**
Then someone grabbed a marker.

On the wall, they wrote:

**"I deserved better. But I'm still here."**

Another added:

"I'm not broken—I'm building."

A third scribbled:

"Sometimes I dissociate in math class. That's not sin. That's survival."

**Bliss smiled.**

"You are not your defense mechanisms.
You're the reason they had to exist.
And now, we build better ones."

They began sharing. Slowly at first. Then wildly.

- One boy's father blamed him for his mother's death

- One girl had been baptized twice just to feel clean

- One student had been outed by a youth pastor and never went back to church

Bliss didn't interrupt. Just nodded. Validated. Let them cry or not cry or laugh when it got weird.

She passed out the next form: "Adulting Skill You Wish Someone Taught You."

Answers included:

- "How to say no without apologizing"

- "How to cry without hiding"

- "How to hug someone without flinching"

**At the end of the night, the whiteboard read:**

**"This Is What Reparenting Looks Like"**

- Sitting in a circle with strangers who let you feel
- Writing the rules you wish you grew up with
- Getting a Capri Sun and a group hug after naming your trauma

One kid lingered after the others left. He asked:

"You think I'm fixable?"

Bliss looked him dead in the eyes.

"Baby, you were never broken.
You just weren't believed."

**Velma's Exhibit of the Erased**

**POV: Velma Houston**
**Setting: Dusty Springs Museum of Resistance – "The Erased Room"**
**Time: Sunday, 9:30 a.m.**

The doors opened slowly.
Soft light. Low hum. Gospel chords woven with field recordings.
The sound of memory catching its breath.

This wasn't a gallery.

This was a sacred damn resurrection.

Velma walked through her curated masterpiece wearing gloves, pearls, and the holy conviction of a woman who survived 40 years of lies and had **organized every damn file cabinet into the afterlife.**

The room was sectioned like a soul dissected gently.

## The Disappeared Voters Wall
— 126 names that had been purged from rolls during the Cain administration.
Each one accompanied by a short bio, a voter selfie, and a line that read:

*"Erased by system. Remembered by kin."*

## The Suppressed Sermons Booth
— Audio tapes of church leaders who spoke out and were "relocated."
One included Pastor Ruth's banned 1997 sermon titled *"Jesus Flipped Tables, So Why Can't I?"*
Visitors could listen via headphones. Some wept. Some stood and shouted "Amen."

## The Portraits with No Names Section
— Mugshots of residents who were arrested, harassed, or "forgotten" during housing protests, gentrification raids, and school board sit-ins.
Velma didn't just post their photos.

She restored their *faces*—smiles, jobs, families, futures. And where names were missing, she simply wrote:

"This person mattered. Help us find them."


**The Room of Receipts**
— Screens lining one full wall rotated through thousands of leaked texts, fake invoices, offshore donations, and burner phone logs.

Above it, gold script read:

**"Truth Was Always an Archive. Y'all Just Didn't File It Right."**


**A group of high schoolers toured quietly.**
One paused at the digital guestbook.

She typed:

*"I found my uncle's name. I thought he just ghosted us. He didn't. They made him disappear."*

Velma whispered behind her:

"Now he's back. And we gon' say his name loud."


**In the final corner:**
A mirror. Just a mirror.
Etched across the top:

**"You're the Author of What Comes Next."**

Velma explained it to a young intern.

"People leave crying. Not because they're broken.
Because they just saw their own power reflected for the first time."


Later that night, she sat alone in the exhibit, eyes on a candlelit photo of a young woman labeled "Unknown Protestor, 2003."

"You were never erased. They just ran out of lies."


## Tyrone's Homecoming Hackathon

**POV: Tyrone Dupree**
**Setting: The Liberation Tech Hub – Newly Opened "Second Circuit" Wing**
**Time: Monday, 8:01 a.m.**


The paint was still drying on the outside wall.
It read:

**"No More 404 Futures."**
*A tech lab for returning citizens, system survivors, and anyone the algorithm forgot.*

Inside, Tyrone prepped a whiteboard as his first cohort filed in— ex-cons, code curious teens, single mothers with ankle monitors, and one grandfather who introduced himself as "Ctrl+Alt+Papaw."


**Tyrone didn't start with HTML.**
He started with this:

"Prison didn't break you.
It paused your download.

Today, we install the update."


**The first exercise?**
Everyone got a sticker name badge.

Not just names—roles.
Hacked by hope.

"Cassandra – UX Disruptor (formerly drug charge)"
"Malik – Server Whisperer (two-time parole warrior)"
"June – Database Queen (reformed credit card swiper)"
"James 'J-Rack' – BitCoin Bandit Turned Budget Analyst"


They started by coding a community-led **Court Translator App**:

- Takes legalese and outputs plain English

- Highlights predatory phrases

- Adds a "Bullsh*t Probability Meter" (rated 1 to 5 gavels)


By noon, the coffee machine was busted and everyone was yelling "merge conflict!" like it was church call-and-response.

Tyrone? He was home.

"Y'all ain't criminals.
You're **debuggers.**
You see the flaw in the system 'cause you lived in the damn glitch."

**One of the students paused.**

"Why teach us this? You could be rich in San Fran right now."

Tyrone smiled.

"Because I'd rather be free in Dusty Springs.
And I want y'all free too. Not just out of prison—**out of shame.**"

**They built:**

- **Clean Slate Sync** – A system to help returning citizens auto-update employment databases with expungements

- **CourtDate+** – Calendar reminders, bus routes, public defenders who *actually call back*

- **ParolePal** – A chatbot that answers "Can I go to my cousin's wedding if my PO hasn't replied?" with legally safe sass

As the day ended, a student named June asked:

"So, like... do we count as developers now?"

Tyrone leaned against the terminal.

"Nah.
You count as **revolutionaries with root access.**"

**Nana's Final Sermon—on a Street Corner, Not a Pulpit**

**POV: Nana May Jackson**
**Setting: Dusty Springs – Ruins of Pastor Ricky's Former Church**
**Time: Monday, 6:59 p.m. (Golden Hour)**

The cross on top had long since toppled.
The stained glass was shattered.
But the steps of Pastor Ricky's former megachurch? Still intact.
Still watching.
Perfect for a sermon.

Nana stepped up in her signature red trench, sensible boots, and no microphone. She didn't need amplification. She had legacy.

The crowd? Mixed.

- Ex-members of Ricky's congregation

- Survivors of his spiritual scams

- Young activists holding signs that read:

**"Holiness ≠ Hostility"**
**"God Don't Need a Building—Just Receipts"**

**Nana cleared her throat. Looked at the ruin behind her. Spoke like a blues chord.**

"You can build a church so big it touches clouds.
But if it don't touch people—it's just a tower of lies."

**Silence fell like prayer beads hitting a hardwood floor.**

She stepped down one stair.

"You ever been told your suffering was a test?
Ever been told to tithe your last dollar, but couldn't get a ride to the doctor?"

One older man shouted, "Every damn Sunday!"

Nana nodded.

"Then you know the truth.
Some folks build temples to trap us—not to free us."

**She gestured behind her.**

"This place was holy in budget only.
It was never about God.
It was about control, shame, and looking righteous on
Instagram."

**Someone from the crowd asked, "So what now?"**

She raised her chin.

"Now? We un-church the trauma.
We de-program the doctrine of 'suffer and smile.'

Now? We build community centers instead of confession
booths.
And call that holy."

**A few clapped. Then more. A ripple turned into a roar.**

A young girl stepped forward, trembling.

"I used to come here every week. Thought it was my fault I got
hurt."

Nana reached out. Held her hand.

"Baby, that wasn't God. That was a man in a costume.
You were always sacred. You were always enough."

**She turned to the crowd again.**

"I'm not your mayor forever.
But I will always be your witness.

If you build something here—make it honest.
Make it open.
And don't name it after me.
Name it after what we survived."

**At that moment, the golden hour kissed the bricks.**
Someone raised a sign that read:

**"This Ground is Redeemed by Truth."**

Nana stepped down, the sermon done.

**Dusty Springs Day – Ratchet, Righteous, and Rebuilt**

**POV: Ensemble (Multiple characters in rotation)**
**Setting: Downtown Dusty Springs – Fully Reopened,**
**Reclaimed, Reimagined**
**Time: Saturday, 2:00 p.m. until somebody calls the fire**
**marshal**

**The street had been renamed. Officially.**

**"Freedom Boulevard (formerly Cain Street)"**

Painted on the asphalt in ten-foot letters:

**WE BUILT THIS SH*T BACK BETTER**

No one argued. Even the city clerk smiled when they filed the paperwork.

## POV: Bliss Monroe

She was at the new **Community Joy Tent**, handing out affirmation slaps in sticker form:

- "Healing Is Ghetto and Glorious"
- "Boundaries Are Sexy"
- "Accountability Isn't Cancel Culture—It's Culture Culture"
- "Your Trauma Isn't an Excuse, But It Explains the Hell Outta You"

Next to her sat the "Breakup Booth"—write a letter to your former toxic belief and ceremonially shred it. The line? Wrapped around the juice truck.

## POV: Tyrone Dupree

Running the **Liberation Arcade**—where every game was political education in disguise.

- "Gerrymander Gauntlet"
- "Zoning Thieves: Developer Edition"
- "POC PAC-MAN" (He only gets half the funding, still wins.)

Behind him, kids coded on laptops with Grandma tutors. One eight-year-old shouted, "I fixed the database schema!"

Tyrone wiped a tear like it was the Super Bowl.

### *POV: Velma Houston*

Presiding over the **Living Archive Tent.** Residents walked in and recorded their own history—voice, video, whatever they had. No permission needed. No filter applied.

Above the tent flapped a banner:

### "No More Missing Pages"

She handed a mic to an old protestor named Ms. Cleotha, who hadn't spoken publicly since 1974.

"Say what you need to say, sugar. The truth is rent-free now."


### *POV: Nana May Jackson*

In a lawn chair. Sipping sweet tea. Wearing sunglasses and a sash that read:

### "Former Mayor. Current Problem."

People came up to thank her. She waved them off.

"This ain't about me. It's about you finally knowing you were always the damn blueprint."

When a teen asked what her next move was, she said:

"I'm opening a dominatrix-themed fitness studio for post-menopausal queens.
Called 'Whip It Real Good.' First class is free if you bring a receipt from a city council donation."


### The final act?

A gospel drag show, hosted by the artist formerly known as Brother Ezekiel, now slaying as Mother Rebuke-a-Lot. Their performance of "This Little Light of Mine" turned into a literal pyrotechnic sermon. Even the skeptical Baptists danced. They learned to truly follow in His teachings and to love everyone, even those they didn't currently understand. They are happily learning though.

The final act was nothing short of miraculous: a gospel drag show led by Mother Rebuke-a-Lot, once Brother Ezekiel, now radiant in sequins and scripture. As the opening chords of "This Little Light of Mine" soared through the air, the pews—usually so rigid—softened. Elders who'd spent decades side-eyeing difference found themselves clapping along, some even wiping away tears. It was as if, for a moment, the walls between altar and dancefloor vanished and the congregation became a chorus of true acceptance.

The church, once wary, embraced their drag and LGBTQ siblings, recognizing in them the living, loving spirit Jesus had preached—unconditional welcome, radical kindness. By the final verse, they didn't just tolerate; they celebrated, having finally learned to love every neighbor exactly as they are.

**As the sun set, the crowd gathered under the restored Dusty Springs clocktower.**

Bliss, Tyrone, Velma, and Nana stood together.
Each lit a torch and handed it to a kid under 13.

No speeches.

Just this inscription carved into the base:

**"We were never powerless. Just unorganized."**

And someone shouted:

"Next year's gonna be bigger!"

To which Nana replied:

"Next year? Baby, we're franchising this sh*t."

**[End of Chapter 16.]**

# Epilogue: Dust Don't Settle Here

**POV: Omniscient Whisperer (a little Nana, a little narrator, a little ancestor)**
**Setting: Dusty Springs – Six Months Later**

Dusty Springs was breathing again. The air felt cleaner, the Wi-Fi was free, and the new community-owned grocery store had a kale selection that would make a Californian weep. Hope wasn't just a hammer anymore; it was a blueprint, and the people were building. The Liberation Center, built on the ashes of Cain Holdings, buzzed with the sound of teenagers coding apps designed to dismantle systemic inequality.

The town's saviors had settled into new roles, not as rulers, but as resources. Bliss Monroe's 'Reclaim & Reparent' program had gone national. Velma Houston secured a grant for a mobile archive truck called "Truth on Wheels" , and Tyrone Dupree launched FreedomStack, a full suite of open-source civic tech for other marginalized towns to use.

And Nana May Jackson? She hadn't run for re-election, officially passing the torch. She had "retired" to her porch, her garden, and her private "consulting" business where the safe word was now "subpoena". She was no longer in office, but she remained in orbit—a gravitational force of truth and tenacity.

Dusty Springs was still imperfect, still recovering, still complicated. But now, it fought back.

But in a world run on power and profit, a town that gets free isn't a success story; it's a threat to a balance sheet hundreds of miles away.

In a sterile, glass-walled boardroom in Atlanta, two men in exquisitely tailored suits looked at a holographic map of Dusty Springs. They were Julian and Marcus Vance, the billionaire brothers behind Prosperity Ascendant, a development firm that bought towns the way other people bought shoes.

"The assets are prime for acquisition," Julian said, his voice devoid of emotion. "The previous local obstacles—Cain, Walls— have been neutralized".

"But the infrastructure is now community-owned," Marcus countered, zooming in on the co-op. "The new mayor is one of them. They've built a digital fortress with that 'Truth Engine' nonsense. We can't bribe our way in".

Julian smiled, a chilling, razor-thin expression. "Then we don't buy the town. We break it".

He brought up a new file. It showed a charismatic, media-savvy preacher from Texas, Reverend Prophet Ezekiel Storm, whose sermons against "woke governance" had gone viral.

"We'll fund a challenger who speaks their language but serves our interests," Julian explained. "We'll back him with a national coalition of megachurches. We'll launch a misinformation campaign that makes the last election look like a bake sale. We'll call their progress 'moral decay.' We'll turn their 'liberation' into a threat".

He zoomed in on a picture of Nana, sitting on her porch, laughing.

"And we'll start with the one who lit the match," Julian said. "We'll sue her. For defamation, for moral terrorism, for everything. We'll bury her in legal fees and bad press. We will make the people of Dusty Springs believe their savior was actually their destroyer".

Marcus looked at the map, at the small, defiant town that had dared to rebuild itself. "And if they fight back?"

Julian's smile widened. "Good. A righteous fight makes for a much more profitable story when we win".

The dust hadn't settled. A new storm was gathering.

**End. For Now.**

**Book 2 Coming Soon...**

# Acknowledgments

To everyone who ever told me, "You can't write that"—
You were the wind beneath my desire.

To the organizers, whistleblowers, caretakers, and chaos coordinators out here building futures in stolen land and Wi-Fi deserts—**this one's for you.**

To every Black elder who held the door open with one foot while carrying a casserole in one hand and a voter registration form in the other—**you are the prototype.**

To the real-life Nanas, Aunties, Tias, Bubbes, Lolas, and Big Mamas who could run a country with nothing but a purse full of receipts and a switch—**thank you for raising hell *and* us.**

To queer activists, trans disruptors, neurodivergent weirdos, and the kinfolk doing liberation work in places where it's illegal to have nuance—**keep flipping tables. This book is your confetti.**

To every corrupt pastor, politician, and nonprofit executive who inspired our villains—**I owe you zero royalties but all of my material.**

To the educators and librarians sneaking banned books into backpacks:
You're the real underground railroad of imagination.

To the ancestors who whispered plot twists at 3am—**I heard you. I wrote it down. I kept it snarky.**

To my ADHD—thank you for turning hyperfocus into a superpower and deadlines into motivational fiction.

And finally:
To the readers who stayed for the gospel drag, the digital rebellion, the senior citizen dominatrix, and the trauma-informed

town hall—

**You are the reason this story doesn't end here.**
**You are Dusty Springs.**
**And baby, we just got rezoned.**

# About the Authors

## Jordan Wright, M.Ed.

Jordan Wright is a lifelong educator, technologist, and storyteller who believes that comedy and chaos are essential ingredients for social progress. With a master's degree in education and a suspicious number of opinions about local government, Jordan writes fiction that flips the script on power, politics, and small-town pettiness. When not dismantling systems (or teaching others to do so), Jordan is probably drinking strong coffee and writing under at least three different pseudonyms. This is not an accident.

## Ibrahim Roble

Ibrahim Roble is an author, beta reader, and editor based in Kenya, with an affinity for stories that unmask hypocrisy, spark laughter, and champion underdogs. A trained electronics technician and unapologetic computer nerd, Ibrahim brings sharp wit, cultural insight, and a global lens to every project he touches. When he isn't rescuing manuscripts from the brink or building the perfect tech rig, you'll find him buried in novels, scheming up new plot twists, or fixing what others said couldn't be fixed.

.

www.ingramcontent.com/pod-product-compliance
Lightning Source LLC
Chambersburg PA
CBHW051938220626
47052CB00004B/706